HEBREW

ALEPHBETS

By: Yow'ab Ben-Yahweh

יואב בן יהוה

Advanced Edition

This is a work of non-fiction. Any relevance to any other work portrayed throughout this work, is solely from the research of the author. This work is not to be considered as doctrine, but a means of furthering your studies as you grow closer to the God of ישראל, יהוה.

All Bible scriptures and/or quotations are taken from the King James Version of the Holy Bible, unless stated otherwise.

Grateful and glorious acknowledgments and Praises are made to יהוה בן יהוה for enabling me with the necessary intelligence to construct such a piece of work, and to all those who help in the producing of this work.

Table of Contents

<u>*INTRODUCTION*</u>

So, what is this system of the Hebrew Aleph-bets? The Hebrew Aleph-bets contains twenty-two letters or Authioth. It is said that the Hebrew language came directly from God, יהוה, Himself. It contains secrets that were preserved by the initiated. They contain the precise plan of the principles of creation. Each letter (or auth) is a crystallization of one of the aspects of manifestation of the divine word. Each letter corresponds to a number, which places it in a numerical hierarchy, a hieroglyph as a visual representation in form, and a symbol that makes it connect to other letters. Each letter is thus connected to the creative forces in the universe. They express themselves on three levels: one level is archetypical and runs from the first to the ninth letter; the second level is one of manifestation and runs from the tenth to the eighteenth letter, and the third is a cosmic level and runs from the nineteenth to the twenty-second letter.

The Hebrew Aleph-bets is a unique and distinctive set of characters or letters with spiritual and numerical values. The Hebrew Aleph-bets, through study, will reveal a great wealth of knowledge. They are more than just your normal set of alphabets, when place together in various combinations they go further than the original meaning of the combinations of letters, they tell a deep and contrast story. The 22 Hebrew letters (aleph bets) which comprise the original Hebrew language are also referred to individually as Hebrew characters and each of the Hebrew characters is words. The characters (letters or words) can be studied through the use of the Strong's Exhaustive Concordance, Holy Bible (KJV), Bible Dictionaries, College Dictionaries, Synonym Finders, and various Hebrew literature and reference books. All of the Hebrew characters are in fact special within themselves. They are the holy words and tools Almighty God, יהוה. Each of the 22 Hebrew letters or characters (א,ב etc.), symbolizes a particular quality, a trait, a personality, a disposition, an attribute, a capacity or status and a reputation. In actuality you can say that they are all an aggregate of distinctive moral and ethical qualities, that form the nature of you (the person) in reference to your behavior (1 Peter 1:15-16). This behavior of how one is to behave can be learned through the study of the Hebrew Aleph-bets that make up your particular Hebrew Name. It is here that your Hebrew Name becomes all-important (Proverbs 22:10).

The Hebrew language is written from right to left and contains 22 letters or characters. There are five additional Hebrew characters that take on a different form when they appear at the end of a word. These letters are known as Final Letters or Sofet. The Hebrew Aleph-bets are especially distinguishable from any other alphabet. The individual letters, their equivalent of the Aleph-bets are all divinely ordained and loaded with meaning.

THE HEBREW ALEPH-BETS

LETTER	NAME	SPELLIN	PRONUNC	VALUE
א	Aleph	אלף	aw'-lef	1; 1000
ב	Beyth	בית	bayth	2
ג	Giymel	גמל	ghee'-mel	3
ד	Daleth	דלת	daw'-leth	4
ה	Hé	הא	hay	5
ו	Wav	וו	wawv	6
ז	Zayin	זין	zah-yin	7
ח	Cheyth	חית	khayth	8
ט	Teyth	טית	tayth	9
י	Yod	יד	yode	10
כ	Kaph	כף	caf	20
ל	Lamed	למד	law'-med	30
מ	Mem	מם	mame	40
נ	Nun	נון	noon	50
ס	Samek	סיך	saw'-mek	60
ע	'Ayin	עין	ah'-yin	70
פ	Pé, Phe	פה	pay, fay	80
צ	Tsaddi	צדי	tsaw-day	90
ק	Qowph	קוף	cofe	100
ר	Resh	ריש	raysh	200
ש	Shin	שין	sheen	300
ת	Thav	תו	thawv	400
ך	Kaph Sofet	כף סיך	caf so-fet	500
ם	Mem Sofet	מם סיך	mame so-fet	600
ן	Nun Sofet	נון סיך	noon so-fet	700
ף	Phe	פה	fay	800

| צ | *Tsaddi* | צ ד י ס י ף | *tsaw-day* | *900* |

LETTER	PRONUNCIATION
א Aleph	silent letter
ב Beyth	like b in Boy
ג Giymel	like g in Gold
ד Daleth	like d in Door
ה Hé	like h in House
ו Wav	like w in Wine
ז Zayin	like z in Zeal
ח Cheyth	like ch in baCH
ט Teyth	like t in Tall
י Yod	like y in Yes
כ Kaph	like k in Kind
ל Lamed	like l in Love
מ Mem	like m in Master
נ Nun	like n in Now
ס Samek	like s in Sun
ע Ayin	silent letter
פ Pé	like p in People
צ Tsaddi	like ts in nuTS
ק Qowph	like k in Kite
ר Resh	like r in Rich
ש Shin	like sh in SHape
ת Thav	like t in Tall

<u>CHAPTER 1</u>
<u>ALEPH</u>
[aw'-lef]
א ל ף
Symbolic: Ox Numerical Value: 1 and 1,000

Aleph is the symbolic ox, with a numerical value of one and 1,000; it represents the strength, unity, love, and the oneness of י ה ו ה , for it is the spirit that unifies consciousness. By Aleph being the first of the Hebrew Alephbets, it represents the first of all firstborn belonging to י ה ו ה ; the purifying power of the Qodesh Ruach. Aleph is triune; 3 in 1—Father, Son, and G-Host—it has a positive Yod in the upper right segment, a negative Yod in the lower left segment, and a Wav as the center pillar for balance between the two Yod's. The positive Yod is the ascension of י ש ר א ל as the ruler of this planet, it is also the upper world of Adam Chochmah: Promordial Black Man, prototype for all humanity; changing from human to super-human, transforming that sexual energy into spiritual energy: "The Ether (Deuteronomy 10:11)." The negative Yod represents י ש ר א ל going astray from the Laws of י ה ו ה , and descending into the lower nature, into a state of unconsciousness, to undergo a 6,000 year deep sleep under the rulership of Satan. Wav as being the center pillar of balance between the two Yod' s serves as י ה ו ה 's loving mercy for His royal priesthood to turn away from their wicked and defiled ways and seek His face so that He will heal the land that was promised to our forefathers (2 Chronicles 7:14).

The image of Aleph is an ox. The ox indicates plowing, the penetration of the earth (the female) by the plow (the male). It has clear sexual meaning. The penetration can also be seen as the Divine Spirit descending into the primeval waters, which it penetrates and impregnates. As a symbol, Aleph represents unity, origin, power, continuity and stability. On the human level, Aleph represents Divine Man. By the form of this letter, it indicates its function as a link between the upper and the lower world, heaven and earth. Aleph as unity, contains in itself duality, as it is also seen in its form. It links the primeval source with everything that emanates from it. The numerical value of Aleph is 111 (א [1]+ל [30]+ף [80]=111). The number 111 contains the trinity, and it is also the constant of the magic square of six. 111=1+10+100. In this sense, Aleph contains the One in units, in tens, and in hundreds. Symbolically this means that Aleph combines the Divine, the Spirituel, and the Physical world. Or, 1 is the Point, the Ayin Soph Aur (The Unlimited Light); 10 is the Tree of life with its 10 sephiroth (The power vessels in which consciousness of the universe expresses itself); and 100 is the physical man in the physical world. The shape of Aleph is composed of two Yod's and a dividing line, which stands for the letter Wav. This gives another numerical value: 10+10+6=26. The number 26 is the value of the Tetragrammaton, י ה ו ה , the name of the LORD God, י ה ו ה .

The Divine Name Elohiym is a fundamental Aleph word that appears in over 2,200 verses. It is based on the root El (God); in which it carries the connotation of strength and might. It is used as the last element in many Biblical names such as Emmanuel (God with us), Samuel (Heard of God), Ezekiel (God will Strengthen) and Daniel (God is my Judge), and as the first element in many titles of God, such as El Elyon and El Shaddai. El is the first element in the Divine Title El Olam used in the Hebrew text of Genesis 21:33. This exact title appears nowhere else in Scripture, but a closely related construct, Elohi Olam, which also means the everlasting God, does appear in Isaiah 40:28:

"Hast thou not known? hast thou not heard, that the everlasting God (Elohi Olam), the LORD, י ה ו ה , the Creator of the ends of the earth, fainteth not, neither is weary? there is no searching of his understanding."

The Hebrew titles used in Genesis (El Olam) and Isaiah (Elohi Olam) are almost identical. They both have the meaning "the everlasting God" in the King James Version of the Bible and each occurs once in the Bible. No similar construct appears anywhere else in the Hebrew Scripture. Furthermore, they are both translated with identical Greek words in the Septuagint, where they are rendered Theos aionios (everlasting God). This then links to the New Testament where this Greek phrase appears in one and only one Book—Romans—where it again is translated as "the everlasting God":

> "Now to him that is of power to stablish you according to my gospel, and the preaching of יהוה בן יהוה בן יהוה, according to the revelation of the mystery, which was kept secret since the world began, But now is made manifest, and by the scriptures of the prophets, according to the commandment of the everlasting God (Theos aionios), יהוה, made known to all nations for the obedience of faith."—Romans 16:25-26

Putting this together, the Divine Title "the everlasting God" appears only three times in the KJV of the Bible, and that this is a faithful representation of text since the Greek and Hebrew titles also appear nowhere else in all of the Scripture. We have therefore a link based on this Divine Title that exemplifies the symbolic meaning of Aleph as expressed in the word El (God). The significance of this link cannot be overstated. It is a link based on Aleph that expresses the Lord's יהוה primary Divine attribute as the everlasting God. It is extremely important to recognize the depth of the symbolic, Aleph-bets, and geometric confluence displayed here. In effect, יהוה has signed and sealed His Word with His Divine Signature as the Everlasting God. The geometry of Aleph integrates with both the message of the text and the symbolic meaning of the first Hebrew Letter! This is an optimal presentation of an absolute truth. A host of human authors could not surpass it if they sat down and devised a circular book out of whole cloth. And since we know this is not how the Bible came to be, we also know that we are witnessing the very Work of יהוה.

Praise His Holy Name now and forever!!!

CHAPTER 2
BEYTH
[bayth]
ב י ת
Symbolic: House Numerical Value:2

Beyth is the symbolic house with a numerical value of two. It represents the duality and plurality of the cosmos created in the image of the Macrocosm: Adam is a microcosm, created in the image of the Macrocosm. Beyth is the first letter in ב י ת (house, family). Beyth is the symbolic house of God י ה ו ה; the temple or your body. י ש ר א ל must keep its body clean in order for י ה ו ה to dwell within. Beyth is also symbolic for "B" or second in command, rank, or quality. Though we may appear to be separate individuals, we are one in the Great Name of י ה ו ה.

The image of the Hebrew letter Beyth is a house, a tent, and dwelling. The house is the dwelling of (the body of) man in the world of duality and illusion. A house also gives protection and shelter (Psalm 23:6; Psalm 55:14). A house is containing form. In the spirituel sense, it contains the Light, and Spirit of the LORD י ה ו ה. Beyth as a house is also a Sanctuary, Temple, and the Gnosis (Knowledge) of the quickening Spirit of י ה ו ה ב ן י ה ו ה ב ן י ה ו ה.

"For we are labourers together with י ה ו ה: ye are God's husbandry, ye are י ה ו ה's building. According to the grace of י ה ו ה which is given unto me, as a wise masterbuilder, I have laid the foundation, and another buildeth thereon. But let every man take heed how he buildeth thereupon. For other foundation can no man lay than that is laid, which is ב ן י ה ו ה. י ה ו ה ב ן י ה ו ה. Know ye not that ye are the temple of י ה ו ה, and that the Spirit of י ה ו ה dwelleth in you?"—1 Corinthians 3:9-11 and 16

The name of the Second Letter is based on the common Hebrew word for house (bayth) found in over 2,000 verses. Its shape in the ancient script represented a tent—the typical house of the Hebrews as they wandered in the wilderness. When rotated, it became the lower case Latin b. As with many words, יהוה presented its meaning in the plain text of the Scripture in the story of Jacob's Ladder: "And he called the name of that place Bethel..." (Genesis 28:19). The third entry in the Tables shows that Bethel is simply the name of the Second Letter followed by the word El (God). Many Christians know Beyth via Bethlehem (House of Bread), where יהוה בן יהוה בן יהוה, the Bread of Life, entered the world to become housed in human flesh. The house symbolizes the ultimate purpose of all reality: to become a dwelling place below for the manifestation of יהוה presence.

This coheres, of course, with the understanding of the consummation of יהוה's Plan of the Ages when He will "dwell with his people" (Revelation 21:3). The Book of Exodus records יהוה's first big step towards fulfilling His Plan to build a "dwelling place below," that is, here on earth. It is in Exodus that יהוה first mentions His Tabernacle as the House of יהוה (Beyth יהוה, Exodus 23:19). This is one of the primary themes of the Second Book which contains the design, given directly from יהוה to Moshe at Mount Sinai, of the pattern of the Tabernacle. Over a third of Exodus (its last fifteen chapters), is devoted to its design and construction; the Book ends with the Tabernacle being filled with the Glory of יהוה, representing His Presence amongst His People, ישראל. This is a major theme of the second book, and it is based on the literal meaning of the name of the second letter, Beyth (House).

יהוה designed the "House of יהוה" as a typological image of יהוה בן יהוה, His Son (Ben, בן) in whom "dwelleth all the fullness of the Godhead bodily" (Colossians 2:9). He is the Word of יהוה who was "made flesh and dwelt (literally tabernacled) amongst us" (St. John 1:14), in perfect agreement with the Type of the Tabernacle which housed the Ten

Commandments, the prototypical Word of יהוה. And just as the Tabernacle was the focus of יהוה's glory on earth which covered it as a bright cloud, so when the Son became flesh, "we beheld his glory, the glory as of the only begotten of the father" (St. John 1:14). There is no end to the depth of the typological correlation between the second letter, the Tabernacle, and the Second Person of the Triune Cycle. יהוה בן יהוה יהוה בן Himself made the typology explicit in the Second Chapter of St. John verses 16 through 22:

"And said unto them that sold doves, Take these things hence; make not my Father's house an house of merchandise. And his disciples remembered that it was written, The zeal of thine house hath eaten me up. Then answered the Jews and said unto him, What sign shewest thou unto us, seeing that thou doest these things? יהוה בן יהוה answered and said unto them, Destroy this temple, and in three days I will raise it up. Then said the Jews, Forty and six years was this temple in building, and wilt thou rear it up in three days? But he spake of the temple of his body. When therefore he was risen from the dead, his disciples remembered that he had said this unto them; and they believed the scripture, and the word which בן יהוה יהוה had said."

The Tabernacle of יהוה is one of the greatest overarching types given in Scripture. It was designed by יהוה as a picture of His whole purpose of creation, first established in the Tabernacle in the Wilderness. This set the stage for יהוה בן יהוה בן as Emmanuel (God with us) which then blossomed into the image of each member of His Body as an individual "Temple of יהוה" (1 Corinthians 3:16) with all the members collectively symbolized as "living stones" "fitly framed together" to form the Body of יהוה בן יהוה, "a holy temple in the body of יהוה יהוה בן יהוה."

Finally, the Book of Revelation consummates this image,

prophetically declaring the time when "the tabernacle of יהוה *is with men, and he will dwell with them, and they shall be his people, and* יהוה *himself shall be with them, and be their God" (Revelation 21:3). This entire typological theme is contained in the Archetype of the House, the essential symbolic power of the Second Letter.*

CHAPTER 3
GIYMEL
[ghee'-mel]
ג מ ל
Symbolic: Camel Numerical Value: 3

Giymel is the symbolic camel with a numerical value of three. It represents Adam Celestial Journey upon the beast as He rises from the Physical Plane to the Astral and on to the Causal; unfolding his consciousness to reach the absolute; י ה ו ה . He travels through the fifty gates of Light until at last He returns to the Highest State of Primordial Consciousness: "Adam Kodman".

Giymel represents the intergalactic travel of the mind from unconscious, to sub-conscious and on to conscious. Giymel represents a rich man running to give alms to a poor man, represented by the letter Daleth. This understanding is essentially "obvious" in two closely related words, Gomel and dal, which means Benefactor and Poor. The words "Gomel and Dal" echo the Aleph-bets sequence "Giymel—Daleth," suggesting Giving to the Poor. Giymel symbolizes the ultimate cheerful giver, so eager to share his abundant wealth that he chases the poor, seeking any chance to give, to bless, and to bestow his riches upon the needy. This understanding coheres with Scripture. In the great alephbetic Psalm 119, the first Giymel Psalm 119:17 states:

"Deal bountifully (ג מ ל , gomal) with thy servant, that I may live, and keep thy word."

Gomel also means "to give" in the sense of to reward, to recompense, or to repay , which can have positive or negative sense depending on what *is deserved.* יהוה *used it in Isaiah 3:8-11 when He said:*

"For Jerusalem is ruined, and Judah is fallen: because their tongue and their doings are against the LORD, יהוה *, to provoke the eyes of his glory. The shew of their countenance doth witness against them; and they declare their sin as Sodom, they hide it not. Woe unto their soul! for they have rewarded (*גמלו *, gamlu) evil unto themselves. Say ye to the righteous, that it shall be well with him: for they shall eat the fruit of their doings. Woe unto the wicked! it shall be ill with him: for the reward (*גמול *, gamul) of his hands shall be given him."*

All these ideas relate to the Holy Spirit, who gives us יהוה *'s abundant gifts, nurtures believers, convicts sinners of their guilt, and comforts them when they repent. Aleph plus Beth equals Giymel, indicating that Giymel represents the Holy Spirit* יהוה בן יהוה בן יהוה *proceeding forth from the Father* יהוה *(Aleph) and the Son* בן יהוה יהוה *(Beyth). And what is the role of the Holy Spirit (or Helper) in olam hazeh? It is threefold: to convict of sin, righteousness, and judgment to come (St. John 16:8). And He will "take what is mine and declare it unto you" (St. John 16:14), bringing true aide to the poor who are trapped behind the Door (Daleth).*

The image of Giymel is a camel. The camel is the riding animal for the desert. It brings the traveler from one place to another, thus linking these two places together. It links Keter and Tiferet, which are connected by the longest path on the Tree of Life. As the camel moves steadily forward, Giymel allows for continuity of movement and form.

CHAPTER 4
DALETH
[daw'-leth]
ד ל ת
Symbolic: Door Numerical Value: 4

Daleth is the symbolic door with a numerical value of four, and it represents materiality, the four physical directions: North, East, South, and West. The Four Hebrew Virtues: Prudence, Temperance, Justice, and Fortitude. Daleth is the doorway to enter the Heavenly Realms of existence. Daleth turns into the directions of the four Metaphysical Worlds of Emanation, Creation, Formation, and Manifestation. It is the foundation upon which to build.

The word for religion is ד ת (dat), which means the "door of the cross;" using the ancient pictographs. The Father (Aleph) sent His Son (Beyth) and by means of the Holy Spirit (Giymel) who makes appeal to the poor and needy to receive the grace of the LORD י ה ו ה , God of Yisrael. As י ה ו ה ב ן י ה ו ה said, "Behold, I stand at the door, and knock: if any man hear my voice, and open the door, I will come in to him, and will sup with him, and he with me" (Revelation 3:20). In regard to an arrogant person י ה ו ה says this: "I and he cannot dwell together." The door to י ה ו ה 's house allows for the humble of spirit to enter. The door itself, the Daleth, is the property of humility and lowliness. Thus the full meaning of the Daleth is the door through which the humble enter into the realization of י ה ו ה 's dwelling place below.

"And when he had opened the fourth seal, I heard the voice of the fourth beast say, Come and see. And I looked, and behold a pale horse: and his name that sat on him was Death, and Hell followed with him. And power was given unto them over the fourth part of the earth, to kill with sword, and with hunger, and with death, and with the beasts of the

Death first appears in Genesis 4. This, along with the fourth seal, that is a natural sequence followed by the first four of the Seven Seals: A Conqueror (Seal 1) causes War (Seal 2) which results in Famine (Seal 3) followed by widespread Death (Seal 4). It is deeply integrated with the Daleth Alephbetic verses. A very similar sequence is associated with the number four seen in the Word of יהוה given through Ezekiel.

The image of Daleth is a door, an entrance, and an exit. For the initiated person Daleth is door or entrance to the inner Light, to Knowledge and Wisdom, to order and structure, and to a new foundation which new can be built.

<u>CHAPTER 5</u>
<u>HÉ</u>
[hay]
ה א
Symbolic: Window Numerical Value: 5

Hé is the symbolic window with a numerical value of five, it represents Spirituality. Hé is the principle of reception. Hé is feminine, passive, and it's the container or formative principle of pattern, form and structure. Hé is the Holy Spirit from whose body the Generations of all creation issue forth. There are two Hé's in HASHEM: the first Hé is the Divine Mother that is impregnated by the Yod and it is the sphere of Binah in the upper world of creation. The final Hé is Malchah in the lower world of action. Hé is the Physical Breath of Life in the Physical World of Duality. Hé symbolizes the fourth element of creation: Earth. Earth represents the manifestation or foundation of the material creation. Hé represents materiality or material nature, which must dwell in harmony with our spiritual nature, for our material being is only an representation of our spiritual being, and therefore, they must have balance. Hé is a virtue, for it is fortitude, we must be strong and courageous to endure to the end victoriously.

"He answered and said, Lo [Hé], I see four men loose, walking in the midst of the fire, and they have no hurt; and the form of the fourth is like the Son of God."—Daniel 3:25

The name of the Fifth Letter is what it sounds like; an interjection demanding attention like "look!" or "behold!" just as we say "hey!" in English and many other languages. It's the simplest of words, requiring only a breath with no articulation. It appears only four times in Scripture; once in Genesis, once in Ezekiel, and twice in Daniel as above where it is rendered Lo. Much more common is the lengthened form hinney, appearing over a thousand times in the Old Testament. יהוה used it in the last Hé verse of the great Alephbetic Psalm 119:

Psalm 119:40: Behold (Hinney), I have longed after thy precepts: quicken me in thy righteousness.

This links to one of its primary roles in Hebrew grammar. When prefixed to a noun, Hé signifies the definite article, the word the. For example, "name" is "shem" (שם) and "the name" is "ha-shem" (השם). It's closely related to the verb hayah (to be, to exist), which יהוה used in four Alephbetic Verses:

Proverbs 31:14: "She is (hayah) like the merchants' ships; she bringeth her food from afar."

Lamentations 1:5: "Her adversaries are (hayah) the chief, her enemies prosper; for the LORD, יהוה, hath afflicted her for the multitude of her transgressions."

Lamentations 2:5: "The Lord יהוה, was (hayah) as an enemy: he hath swallowed up ישראל, he hath swallowed up all her palaces: he hath destroyed his strong holds."

Lamentations 3:14: "I was (hayah) a derision to all my people; and their song all the day."

The Hé prefix also signifies the grammatical conjugation called the hiphil imperative, which indicates causation. יהוה used it this way in most of the Alephbetic Verses, such as these three verses from Psalm 119:35-37:

"Make me to go in the path of thy commandments; for therein do I delight.

Incline my heart unto thy testimonies, and not to covetousness. Turn away mine eyes from beholding vanity; and quicken thou me in thy way."

The Psalmist pleads for י ה ו ה to cause him to go in the path of His commandments, to cause his heart to incline to His testimonies, to cause his eyes to turn from vanity. This is the meaning of the Hiphil imperative conjugation, indicated by the Hé prefix. Hé gives great insight into the meaning of the Divine Name י ה ו ה, the Tetragrammaton, in which Hé appears twice. It contains within itself the three tenses of the verb *hayah* (to be) — past, present, and future—and so carries the sense of both "He who is, was, and will be" and "He who causes things to be." י ה ו ה explicitly proclaimed the eternal meaning of His Name when He described Himself as the Almighty God י ה ו ה, "who is, who was, and who is to come" (Revelation 1:8).

The image of the letter Hé is a window. The letter stems from a root that means "to breathe" in the sense of allowing air and Light. To see and to breathe are two vital parts of life. A window provides light and air to come in. It is an opening for the Light of י ה ו ה to reach us.

CHAPTER 6
WAV
[wawv]

ו ו

Symbolic: Nail or Hook Numerical Value: 6

    Wav is the symbolic nail or hook with a numerical value of six, it represents the six members of the Physical Adam. Therefore Wav is the number of the image of man (the made man land and his activity). Wav is the third letter of HA-SHEM, for it is the movement or activity of Yod moving through Hé . It is the World of Formation. Wav is the Principle of Activity. Wav is the center pillar of balance between the positive and negative Yod's, for both must live in harmony in order to exist (Isaiah 45:7); for if they do not exist in harmony; the whole world will be in total chaos.

    Wav sits on the Sephira Chesed (Mercy) and it represents the movement of Yod into the metaphysical world of formation. Wav is the Divine Mercy and protection of י ה ו ה *. Wav is also the channel that travels from Keter (Crown) into Binah (Understanding). Wav symbolizes the restoration of judgment, the continuity of uniting Heaven with Earth through Chesed and Gevurah; for it is justice. You must stand morally upright on a square (Yesod-Foundation) within a circle in order to rebuild our Holy Nation. Wav is also symbolic for the chemical element of Tungsten; in which it becomes resistant to evil and all ungodliness that corrodes the Mind, Body, and Soul and is completely purified*

    "Let this mind be in you, which was also in בן יהוה בן יהוה יהוה *: Who, being in the form of God, thought it not robbery to be equal with God: But made himself of no reputation, and took upon him the form of a servant, and was made in the likeness of men: And being found in fashion as a man, he humbled himself, and became obedient unto death,*

even the death of the cross."—Philippians 2:6

The name of the sixth letter denotes a nail or hook, as suggested by its shape. It appears thirteen times in Exodus where it describes the hooks holding each curtain to its pillar in the Tabernacle. Wav exemplifies its role in Hebrew grammar. When prefixed to a word, it represents the conjunctive—the Hebrew form of <u>and</u>, <u>also</u>, <u>so</u>, <u>but</u>, and <u>so forth</u>. Wav "hooks" the words and links them together in a sentence. י ה ו ה used it this way in all the Alephbetic Verses. Here are four verses from the great Alephbetic Psalm 119:42-45:

"<u>So</u> shall I have wherewith to answer him that reproacheth me: for I trust in thy word. <u>And</u> take not the word of truth utterly out of my mouth; for I have hoped in thy judgments. <u>So</u> shall I keep thy law continually for ever and ever. <u>And</u> I will walk at liberty: for I seek thy precepts."

י ה ו ה presented no other word in these Alephbetic verses because He designed no other Wav, except for the name of the letter. The Strong's Hebrew Dictionary gives a good number of words that begin with each letter. It's about 400 words each, with Aleph, Mem, and Shin—which are known as the three "Mother Letters"—having the greatest number with over 700 words per Letter. Hé , Zayin, Teyth, and Lamed have much fewer, ranging between 100 and 200 each. Amongst all the letters, Wav is unique. The Strong's Concordance has only ten words that start with it, and most of those are proper nouns of unknown or foreign origin like Vaheb, Vashti, and Vajezatha. This is the only information י ה ו ה gives in the Alephbetic Verses. As a word, Wav means a nail or hook, and 2). Wav signifies the conjunctive in Hebrew grammar. That's it. There are no other Wav words.

Wav, therefore; is י ה ו ה 's symbol of a connector. It's prominent in the seventeen historical books of the Old Testament, it appears as the first letter in all but four books. Wav connects the historical narrative from

Genesis to Malachi. For example, Exodus opens with "And these are the names," and in Leviticus with "And the Lord called," and also Numbers with "And the Lord יהוה spake." Wav carries its meaning as a connector into the words formed when it combines with other Letters. Most notably, it combines with the Lamed prefix-ל -the sign of the prepositions to or for to form the principle letters of the name of the priestly class—לוי (Levi)–based on the verb לוה (lavah) meaning to be joined. It's typical that the Bible gives its etymology at the birth of the progenitor:

"And she conceived again, and bare a son; and said, Now this time will my husband be joined (lavah) unto me, because I have born him three sons: therefore was his name called Levi."—Genesis 29:34

Levi's name forms a lucid word picture. Its final letter is the Yod suffix (sign of me or mine), so his name means to connect to me, which coheres precisely with יהוה's fundamental purpose of Levitical Priests, the mediators who connected ישראל to Him. They prefigured the true High Priest, the "one mediator between יהוה and men, the man יהוה יהוה בן יהוה בן יהוה בן" (1 Timothy 2:5). יהוה בן יהוה connects us with יהוה. Hé is the link between heaven and earth. Leah's words spoken at Levi's birth amplifies this perfectly. She said her husband would be joined to her. This takes us back to the ultimate purpose of all creation revealed with perfect clarity in the consummating Marriage of the Lamb.

יהוה interwove all these ideas in the opening passage of Scripture. Wav first occurs in the Bible as the prefix to the sixth word of Genesis 1:1 where it connects heaven and earth. This is an example of the supernatural coherence of patterns of the whole Bible down to the exact placement and meaning of the individual letters. The sixth letter first occurs as a prefix to the sixth word. It's the twenty-second character of Genesis 1:1 and is prefixed to the sign of the direct object—את—the Aleph Thav (et), derived from יהוה's Capstone Signature AΩ/את. The depth of symbolic convergence here is truly astounding. It reveals the ultimate theological significance of the sixth letter. What's really amazing is that none of this is new. It has been understood for centuries. Much of ancient rabbinic tradition concerning the Aleph-bets placement of Wav indicates two essential connective powers:

1.   By joining heaven and earth it implies the connection between spiritual and physical matters.

2.   Since it occurs as the 22nd letter in the Torah attached to the sixth word, את, it alludes to the creative connection between all of the letters. Wav is therefore the connecting force of the יהוה, the divine "hook" that binds together heaven and earth.

In Genesis 1:1, Wav combines with Aleph Thav—the Sign of the Lord of History, the One Mediator, the Man יהוה בן יהוה בן יהוה, the Living Word—to connect heaven and earth in the most literal sense! (All puns intended). This means that the consummation of all history revealed in the Final Book is prophesied in the pattern of Hebrew letters in the first verse of the First Book! Glory to יהוה in the highest! There is no limit to His Wisdom.

The image of the letter Wav is a nail or hook. Both have the function of fixing something. The nail's function is joining to parts together.

CHAPTER 7
ZAYIN
[zah-yin]

ז י ן

Symbolic: Spear Numerical Value: 7

Zayin is the symbolic spear or weapon, with a numerical value of seven, it represents completion. It signifies the Antithesis to which Adam is exposed. Seven days in a week, Seventh day Shabbat, Seven Heavens, the Seventh Year, and the Seven Elohiym (Archangels). It's the (mark) of י ה ו ה , for it is symbolic for the keeping of Torah and the Shabbat. It is said, he who breaketh HA-TORAH is a transgressor, but he who breaketh the Shabbat is a heathen. Zayin is the sublimation of sexual desire(energy) and transforming it into Spirituel energy.

"And it came to pass, as soon as Gideon was dead, that the children of י ש ר א ל turned again, and went a whoring after Baalim, and made Baalberith their god. And the children of י ש ר א ל remembered not the LORD י ה ו ה , their God, who had delivered them out of the hands of all their enemies on every side."—Judges 8:33-34

The name of the seventh letter denotes a weapon, usually understood as a sword. In modern Hebrew, it means to be armed. This links to the primary theme of fighting that dominates the Seventh Book. It sounds like an English "z" and was drawn as such in the ancient Hebrew scripture. Many Zayin words express the idea of motion—busy buzzing motion. This is particularly evident in the words zavav (buzz) and zevuv (fly). Christians are familiar with the latter from the name Baalzebub (Lord of the flies) which uses the "b" sound of the hard Beyth (b), though the softer "v" sound is more accurate. These words are onomatopoetic (they sound like what they describe), which is why we see the same consonants in English words like busy and buzz. This is the busyness of the world that constantly attacks and distracts us as we struggle to enter into the rest that יהוה offers (Hebrew 4:11), by the Seventh Day Shabbat, the fourth commandment:

"Remember (Zakar) the Shabbat day, to keep it holy. Six days shalt thou labour, and do all thy work: But the seventh day is the Shabbat of the LORD יהוה, thy God: in it thou shalt not do any work, thou, nor thy son, nor thy daughter, thy manservant, nor thy maidservant, nor thy cattle, nor thy stranger that is within thy gates: For in six days the LORD יהוה made heaven and earth, the sea, and all that in them is, and rested the seventh day: wherefore the LORD יהוה blessed the Shabbat day, and hallowed it."—Exodus 20:8-11

The imperative verb in this command – zakar (remember) – is also the primary Zayin word that יהוה used nine times in the Alephbetic verses:

Psalm 25:6: "Remember, O LORD, יהוה, thy tender mercies and thy lovingkindnesses; for they have been ever of old."

Lamentations 3:19: "Remembering mine affliction and my misery, the wormwood and the gall."

Psalm 119:49: "Remember the word unto thy servant, upon which thou hast caused me to hope."

Psalm 119:52: "I remembered thy judgments of old, O LORD, יהוה; and have comforted myself."

Psalm 119:55: "I have remembered thy name, O LORD, יהוה, in the night, and have kept thy law."

Lamentations 1:7: "Jerusalem remembered in the days of her affliction and of her miseries all her pleasant things that she had in the days of old, when her people fell into the hand of the enemy, and none did help her: the adversaries saw her, and did mock at her Shabbats."

Lamentations 3:20: "My soul hath them still in remembrance, and is humbled in me."

Psalm 145:7: "They shall abundantly utter the memory of thy great goodness, and shall sing of thy righteousness."

Psalm 111:4: "He hath made his wonderful works to be remembered: the LORD יהוה, is gracious and full of compassion."

יהוה's extreme emphasis on this one word shows His concern that we remember Him, His Works, and the spiritual meaning of the Seventh Day Shabbat that now is fulfilled in יהוה בן יהוה, our Everlasting Rest:

"Let no man therefore judge you in meat, or in drink, or in respect of an holyday, or of the new moon, or of the Shabbat days: Which are a shadow of things to come; but the body [substance, reality] is of יהוה בן יהוה. יהוה בן."—Colossians 2:16-17

יהוה marked the connection between the Seventh Day and ישראל by placing the final occurrence of the word Shabbat in Bible in this verse from Colossians.

יהוה amplified the idea of remembrance in two Alephbetic verses with the word zamam which means <u>to think</u>, <u>consider</u>, <u>meditate</u>, or <u>plan</u>:

Proverbs 31:16: "She considereth (zamam) a field, and buyeth it: with the fruit of her hands she planteth a vineyard."

Psalm 37:12: "The wicked plotteth (zamam) against the just, and gnasheth upon him with his teeth."

This is what יהוה calls us to do in this busy buzzing world of endless motion. Be still, and know He is God. יהוה בן יהוה בן יהוה must be our meditation and our remembrance all the day long.

The image of the letter Zayin is a sword, spear or weapon in general. The sword is a weapon to attack, to defend, to cut into. Zayin is regarded as the generating and ruling principle over universal movement. In this movement it learns to controls its opposites by the function of will.

<u>CHAPTER 8</u>
<u>CHEYTH</u>
[khayth]
ח י ת
Symbolic: Gate Numerical Value: 8

Cheyth is the symbolic gate with a numerical value of eight, and it represents Divine Protection. It represents the blood of the Passover Lamb. Cheyth signifies a moral and spiritual awareness. It is the reawakening of Spirituel Consciousness, a renewed mind-set.

"The angel of the LORD י ה ו ה *encampeth (chanah) round about them that fear him, and delivereth them."*—Psalm 34:7

The eighth letter represents a gate, hedge, wall, or enclosure. This coheres with its ancient form that looks like two fence poles with two or three rails. It gave rise to the Greek and Latin forms of the Letter H. The number of Cheyth words expressing similar ideas is truly astounding. There really is no other letter with such a dense and consistent grouping of associated ideas. Its symbolic meaning is particularly evident in words that start with Cheyth Beyth, like chov (bosom), chavav (cherish), chavar (friend), chevel (cord), and so forth. Note that Cheyth is pronounced as an "h" with rough breathing, like the "ch" in Bach. י ה ו ה *used four of the words listed in the table in the Cheyth Aleph-betic Verses; one cited above, and these three:*

Proverbs 31:17: "She girdeth (chagar) her loins with strength, and strengtheneth her arms."

Psalm 119:61: "The bands (chevel) of the wicked have robbed me: but I have not forgotten thy law."

Psalm 119:63: "I am a companion (chavar) of all them that fear thee, and of them that keep thy precepts."

These verses establish the fundamental meaning of Cheyth as something that surrounds, binds, and holds things together, both physically as a wall, and socially as friendship and love. It is, therefore, a great joy to see the one word that יהוה used most frequently in the Cheyth Alephbetic verses carries within itself the fundamental message of the Gospel, grace and mercy!

Psalm 111:4: "He hath made his wonderful works to be remembered: the LORD יהוה is gracious (channun) and full of compassion."

Psalm 112:4: "Unto the upright there aristeh light in the darkness: he is gracious (channun), and full of compassion, and righteous.

Psalm 145:8: "The LORD יהוה is gracious (channun), and full of compassion; slow to anger, and of great mercy (chesed)."

In all three verses, gracious appears in conjunction with the Resh word racham (compassion), spelt Resh Cheyth Mem Sofet. In the third verse, יהוה used it in conjunction with another Cheyth word: Chesed meaning mercy, that He also used as the primary word in two other Alephbetic verses:

Psalm 119:64: "The earth, O LORD, יהוה, is full of thy mercy (chesed): teach me thy statutes."

Lamentations 3:22: "It is of the LORD's יהוה mercies (chesed) that we are not consumed, because his compassions (racham) fail not."

Lamentations 3:23: "They are new (chadash) every morning: great is thy faithfulness."

The third verse is consecutive with Lamentations 3:22 and should be read with it. It introduces the word chadash (new) which correlates with the universally recognized symbolic meaning of the Number 8 as New Beginnings. Note the associated word chinnam (free) describes the nature of יהוה 's grace. Putting all this together, we see the essential promise of יהוה and message of the Gospel: We are hedged about on every side with יהוה 's free Mercy and Grace! Now that's the Gospel!

The image of the letter Cheyth is a gate or hedge. Cheyth is the term for the profession of a tailor; and is the action of sewing and implies the making of a garment. In the spirituel sense a robe is the symbol of the physical body. The soul has taken on a physical body like man dresses himself with a garment (Ephesians 6:13-14). Cheyth symbolizes universal equilibrium, the reservoir of energy, the action of breathing the vital breath, the law of attraction and repulsion.

CHAPTER 9

TEYTH

[tayth]

ט י ח

Symbolic: Serpent Numerical Value: 9

Teyth is the symbolic serpent, with a numerical value of nine and it represents completion, balance, and equilibrium. It is the life force in the universe that fragments consciousness. It is equated to the ego, duality, and individualism. It is the Procreative Energy Force of passion, desire, and sensuality in the lower nature that must be transformed into a Spirituel energy force to raise HA-MASHIYACH it is נ חש (nachash: divine—H5172).

"Wherefore also we pray always for you, that our God י ה ו ה would count you worthy of this calling, and fulfil all the good pleasure of his goodness, and the work of faith with power: That the name of our Lord ב ן י ה ו ה י ה ו ה ב ן י ה ו ה may be glorified in you, and ye in him, according to the grace of our God י ה ו ה and the Lord י ה ו ה ב ן י ה ו ה ." —2
Thessalonians 1:11-12

י ה ו ה established the symbolic power of the ninth letter with great clarity. He used the same word tov (good) in thirteen of the Alephbetic verses corresponding to Teyth:

Psalm 25:8: "Good and upright is the LORD י ה ו ה : therefore will he teach sinners in the way."

Psalm 112:5: "A good man sheweth favour, and lendeth: he is gracious, and full of compassion, and righteous"

Lamentations 3:27: "It is good for a man that he bear the yoke in his youth.”

Psalm 119:71: “It is good for me that I have been afflicted; that I might learn thy statutes.”

Lamentations 3:26: “It is good that a man should both hope and quietly wait for the salvation of the LORD יהוה.”

Psalm 119:68: “Thou art good, and doest good; teach me thy statutes.”

Psalm 119:66: “Teach me good judgment and knowledge: for I have believed thy commandments.”

Psalm 145:9: “The LORD יהוה is good to all: and his tender mercies are over all his works.”

Lamentations 3:25: “The LORD יהוה is good unto them that wait for him, to the soul that seeketh him.”

Psalm 119:65: “Thou hast dealt well with thy servant, O LORD, יהוה, according unto thy word.”

Psalm 119:72: “The law of thy mouth is better unto me than thousands of gold and silver.”

Psalm 37:16: “A little that a righteous man hath is better than the riches of many wicked.”

Lamentations 4:9: “They that be slain with the sword are better than they that be slain with hunger: for these pine away, stricken through for want of fruits of the field.”

These verses reveal the primary significance that יהוה invested in Teyth from the beginning. The first occurrence of Teyth in Scripture is in the tov describing יהוה's initial act of creation:

"And יהוה said, Let there be light: and there was light. And יהוה saw the light, that it was good (tov)."—Genesis 1:3-4.

It describes the essence of His work. He used it seven times in the creation account, capping it off with the declaration that everything (et-kol) was very good (tov me'od). Its ninth occurrence is striking because it describes the Tree of the Knowledge of Good (Tov) and Evil (Ra) which plays a very significant role. Note that the word for evil (ra) is a Resh word which is diametrically opposed to Teyth.

These antithetical ideas are represented by the letters ט (Teyth) and ר (Resh) which are like the letters of et-kol (everything), diametrically opposed. The reality of our fallen world we live in, is that these opposites are also inextricably intertwined in constant warfare with each other. There is a hint of this in the name of the ninth letter, Teyth, which it indicates the concept of twisting and assumed by scholars to be based on an ancient word meaning serpent. This links directly to the Tree of the Knowledge of Good and Evil and the origin of evil when Satan told the first lie in violation of the universal law that later would be enshrined in the ninth commandments. It was through his lie and our first parents' disobedience to the word of the Lord יהוה that evil (ra) entered the world that יהוה had created very good (tov me'od). The interplay between the words tov and ra is displayed with great clarity in the story of Saul's persecution of David.

The image of the letter Teyth is the coiling of a serpent. It represents potential power, like serpent before striking. The power has been built up, and is contained, and then released. The power we are speaking of here is spirituel awareness that builds up in man, and is then released to create an heightened awareness in order to remind him of his divine origin.

CHAPTER 10
YOD
[yode]
י ד

Symbolic: Hand Numerical Value: 10

Yod is the symbolic hand, with a numerical value of ten, it also represents the Principle of Force. It is masculine, active, and creative. Yod is the germ, the life, the flame, the cause, the one, and most fundamental of the Hebrew Phallic Emblems. Its numerical is ten and it is to be consider the one containing the ten. From ten, all other numbers are formed in the Kabalah. It is declared that the Yod is in reality three Yod's, of which the first is the beginning, the second is the middle, and third is the end of creation. Its throne is the Sephira Chochmah, from which it goes forth to impregnate Hé , the results of this union is Wav, that manifested in י ה or (YAH), who is the Great Father of all things: the Father of all fathers. Alone Yod symbolizes the ineffable name י ה ו ה .

"Now unto the King eternal, immortal, invisible, the only wise God, י ה ו ה , be honour and glory for ever and ever. Amen."—1 Timothy 1:17

The name of the tenth letter is based on yad (H3027), the Hebrew word for a hand. י ה ו ה established its name in four Alephbetic Verses:

Psalm 119:73: "Thy hands have made me and fashioned me: give me understanding, that I may learn thy commandments."

Proverbs 31:19: "She layeth her hands to the spindle, and her hands hold the distaff."

Lamentations 1:10: "The adversary hath spread out his hand upon all her pleasant things: for she hath seen that the heathen entered into her sanctuary, whom thou didst command that they should not enter into thy congregation."

Lamentations 4:10: "The hands of the pitiful women have sodden their own children: they were their meat in the destruction of the daughter of my people."

The Yod as a hand symbolizes power, might, ability, and authority because with it we handle, control, possess, and manipulate everything in our world. Yad is translated as power twelve times in the King James Version Bible and when יהוה *gave dominion over all creatures to Noah and his sons, he said "into your hand are they delivered." A ruling king has the land under the "power of his hand" and* יהוה *freed* ישראל *from their bondage Egypt "with great power, and with a mighty hand" (Exodus 32:11).* יהוה בן יהוה *asserted His Authority as Divine Messiah when He answered the High Priest saying "Hereafter shall ye see the Son of man sitting on the right hand of power of God,* יהוה *" (Luke 22:69). Scripture always talks about the "work of his hands" as a general metaphor for all that a person does, and in the sense for all* יהוה *'s work in creation, as in the Yod verse above, "Thy hands have made me and fashioned me" (Psalm 119:73).*

This connection between Yod and Action is the basis of its two primary roles in the Hebrew grammar. The Yod prefix signifies the grammatical conjugation called the "third person masculine imperfect" which is how Hebrew conveys the sense of "he does" or "he is doing" as. The Yod Suffix signifies the "first person possessive," the sense of me and mine. This is the basis of the number 10 in the Ten Commandments which is יהוה *'s fundamental guide to telling us how to act (Yod Prefix—Active Hand), with the Tenth Commandment itself, Thou shalt not covet, relating directly to personal possession (Yod Suffix). These ideas are dominant themes of 1 Timothy.*

Yod is the smallest of the Hebrew Aleph-bets. It gave rise to the Greek Iota, called a jot in the KJV of the Bible when יהוה בן יהוה used it as a symbol of the smallest detail of Scripture:

"For verily I say unto you, Till heaven and earth pass, one jot (iota) or one title shall in no wise pass from the law, till all be fulfilled."—Matthew 5:18

The words IOTA and JOT come directly from the Hebrew letter YOD, with the I and J corresponding to the Y, and the T corresponding to the D (both dentals). The smallest of letters is the symbol of the greatest of powers. Rabbinic tradition sees this as teaching that "greatness lies in humble self-effacement."

The image of the letter Yod is hand with stretched fingers. The hand is a symbol of power, of creative and directed energy that maintains individual existence. The open hand is the symbol of the microcosms and the microcosmic man. The closed is a symbol of the Center, The Unity out of which everything emanated, and around which everything revolves. Yod is the smallest letter of the Hebrew Aleph-bets, and as a point it refers the primal vibration of the universe.

CHAPTER 11

KAPH

[caf]

כ ף

Symbolic: Hollow Hand Numerical Value: 20

Kaph is the symbolic hollow hand, with a numerical value of twenty and it represents power, authority, and י ה ו ה 's supreme rulership over the cosmos.

    "And Solomon stood before the altar of the LORD י ה ו ה in the presence of all the congregation of י שׂ ר א ל , and spread forth his hands (kaph) toward heaven: And he said, LORD י ה ו ה , God of י שׂ ר א ל , there is no God like thee, in heaven above, or on earth beneath, who keepest covenant and mercy with thy servants that walk before thee with all their heart."—1 Kings 8:22

    The name of the eleventh letter denotes the palm or hollow of the hand. י ה ו ה established its name in one of His Aleph-betic verses such as Proverbs 31:20:

    "She stretcheth out her hand (kaph) to the poor; yea, she reacheth forth her hands to the needy."

    This exhibits Kaph as the symbol of the Open/Giving hand extended to the poor. It contrasts with Yod as the symbol of the Active/Grasping Hand. Kaph also represents receiving, as when we hold our hands open to י ה ו ה and pray for His blessings like Solomon did when he lifted the name of the eleventh letter in the figure of his palms unto the Lord י ה ו ה .

    There is a strong link between the verses above; they both use the verb parash, translated as "spread forth" in 1 Kings 8:22 and "stretcheth" in

Proverbs 31:20. Kaph also denotes a spoon (1 Kings 7:50), since it is similar to the palm of a hand, and the sole of the foot as when יהוה put David's enemies "under the soles (kaph) of his feet" (1 Kings 5:3). Kaph is one of the five letters known as sofets (ך) when written at the end of a word.

Solomon spoke his prayer at the dedication of the Temple he built after being established (kun) as King upon the throne (kissey) of ישראל. This fulfilled the promise יהוה had made to his father David:

"And the LORD יהוה said unto him, I have heard thy prayer and thy supplication, that thou hast made before me: I have hallowed this house, which thou hast built, to put my name there for ever; and mine eyes and mine heart shall be there perpetually. And if thou wilt walk before me, as David thy father walked, in integrity of heart, and in uprightness, to do thee, and wilt keep my statutes and my judgments: Then I will establish (kun) the throne (kissey) of thy kingdom upon ישראל for ever, as I promised to David thy father, saying, There shall not fail thee a man upon the throne (kissey) of ישראל."—1 Kings 9:3

This is the climax of the entire historical sequence. The word kissey (throne) distinguishes the Eleventh Book from all others. Obviously, it needs no explanation. First Kings is the book that established בן יהוה יהוה as our incomparable King sitting on the Throne of His Glory. This links us to the third word that came to prominence at the dedication of the Temple when יהוה revealed His presence by filling it with a cloud of glory:

"And it came to pass, when the priests were come out of the holy place, that the cloud filled the house of the LORD יהוה, So that the priests could not stand to minister because of the cloud: for the glory (kavod) of the LORD יהוה had filled the house of the LORD יהוה.—

1 Kings 8:10"

This verse exemplifies one of the most significant Kaph words:

Psalm 145:11: "They shall speak of the glory (kavod) of thy kingdom, and talk of thy power."

And speak they did! The fame of Solomon's Kingdom spread far and wide:

"And there came of all people to hear the wisdom of Solomon, from all kings of the earth, which had heard of his wisdom."—1 Kings 4:34

Most notable amongst his visitors was the Queen of Sheba. She simply could not believe the stories that were being told of Solomon's Kingdom, so she came to check it out for herself:

"And she said to the king, It was a true report that I heard in mine own land of thy acts and of thy wisdom. Howbeit I believed not the words, until I came, and mine eyes had seen it: and, behold, the half was not told me: thy wisdom and prosperity exceedeth the fame which I heard. Happy are thy men, happy are these thy servants, which stand continually before thee, and that hear thy wisdom. Blessed be the LORD יהוה, thy God, which delighted in thee, to set thee on the throne (kissey) of ישראל: because the LORD יהוה loved ישראל for ever, therefore made he thee king, to do judgment and justice."—1 Kings 10:6-9

Solomon's wisdom and glory are truly proverbial; יהוה בן יהוה *יהוה בן mentioned both. Rabbi Munk (Wisdom of the Hebrew Alphabet, pg 138) gave his Jewish insight into the symbolic meaning of Kaph and how it relates to the Mem word malkuth (kingdom).*

The Lamed is a majestic Letter, towering above the other letters from its position in the center of the Aleph-bets. Thus it symbolizes the King of Kings, the Supreme Ruler. On one side Lamed is flanked by the Kaph which alludes to the kiseh hakavod, י ה ו ה 's Throne of Glory, while on its other side stands Mem, the Attribute of malkuth, י ה ו ה 's Kingship. Together, these three letters spell מ ל ך (Melek, King).

The image of the letter Kaph is the palm of the hand. It refers to the acceptance of whatever is coming to you. When you have the cycles of the Wheel of Life, and good and bad luck, you will accept them both because you know that good and bad are only relative terms, and have no existence on their own. It is important to understand their inherent energies or power, and why they arise in life. Acceptance of both good and bad things in life gives the opportunity not to spill any energy, as would be done by going against the laws of the universe. It brings you more power. By holding your own power and strength, in the palm of your hand, you can learn to use it in the appropriate way. Kaph also symbolizes the divine force we receive, hold, channel and direct through ourselves.

CHAPTER 12
LAMED
[law'-med]
ל מ ד
Symbolic: Ox-Goad Numerical Value: 30

Lamed is the symbolic ox-goad with a numerical value of thirty, and it represents discipline. For one must discipline the lower nature in Torah in order to overcome the desires and appetites of the ego. We must learn and teach the virtues and morals of Holy Life to stand upright as the King of kings.

"Holding fast the faithful word as he hath been taught, that he may be able by sound doctrine both to exhort and to convince the gainsayers. For there are many unruly and vain talkers and deceivers, specially they of the circumcision: Whose mouths must be stopped, who subvert whole houses, teaching things which they ought not, for filthy lucre's sake."—Titus 1:9-11

The twelfth letter represents the rod of the teacher. It is the "pointer" letter which is why its taller than the others. Its ancient form pictured a shepherd's staff, ox goad, or pointer. It was essentially identical to our modern "L" and corresponds quite naturally to the rod in the classic image of the Good Shepherd. As a verb, Lamed means both to teach and to learn. It is the root of Talmud, the name of the compendium of Jewish learning and tradition. Just as the role of the teacher is to point to the truth, the Lamed prefix indicates such prepositions as <u>to</u>, <u>for</u>, <u>towards</u>, and <u>according to</u> in Hebrew grammar. י ה ו ה used it in most of the corresponding Alephbetic verses, such as the three consecutive verses that begin the Lamed section of Psalm 119:89-91:

"FOR ever (L'olam), O LORD , י ה ו ה , thy word is settled in heaven.

Thy faithfulness is UNTO all generations (L'dor vador): thou hast established the earth, and it abideth.
They continue this day ACCORDING TO thine ordinances (L'mishpateka): for all are thy servants."

Besides demonstrating the role of Lamed in Hebrew grammar, all three of these verses emphasize its symbolic meaning as the Faithful Rod of the Supreme Ruler by which all things are settled and established so that they remain, abide, and continue. Jewish tradition teaches that this is why Lamed stands tall in the center of the Mem word melek (king), as explained by Rabbi Munk in the twelfth chapter of his book *The Wisdom of the Hebrew Alphabet* titled *Lamed: The Symbol of Teaching and Purpose.* It is particularly significant that Munk interwove his explanation of Lamed with the symbolic meanings of Kaph and Mem using exactly the same meanings that we have seen to be profoundly integrated with the structure of the Bible. The Lamed is a majestic Letter, towering above the other Letters from its position in the center of the Alphabet. Thus it symbolizes the King of Kings, the Supreme Ruler. On one side Lamed is flanked by the Kaph which alludes to the kiseh hakavod, יהוה 's Throne of Glory, while on its other side stands Mem, the Attribute of malkuth, יהוה 's Kingship. Together, these three Letters spell Melek (King).

We have, therefore, a complete integration of the traditional rabbinic understanding of the meaning of all three of these Letters – Kaph, Lamed, Mem – with what we have discovered from the Alephbetic Verses, this is fully integrated with the geometric structure of Lamed in the most astounding ways. Furthermore, this integrates with the maximized distribution of the word melek (king), corresponding to the Lamed at its center.

The Lamed prefix combines with the Kaph suffix (a sign of you or yours) to form the word lekha meaning to you or for you. Likewise, the

Lamed prefix combines with the Yod suffix (a sign of me or mine) to form the word li meaning to me or for me. י ה ו ה used these words in three Alephbetic Verses: Psalm 119:94-95:

"I am thine (Lekha ani), save me; for I have sought thy precepts. The wicked have waited for me (li qivu) to destroy me: but I will consider thy testimonies."

The phrase "I am thine" uses the Aleph word ani (I) and literally reads "To thee I am." The word order of the second verse was also changed in translation; the actual Hebrew begins with Li qivu (For me they have waited). י ה ו ה used a similar word in Psalm 34:11:

"Come ye (Lekhu) children, hearken unto me: I will teach you the fear of the LORD י ה ו ה ."

This verse is particularly rich. It contains three fundamental Lamed words, including the name of the twelfth letter. This verse is integrated with the exact sequence of Books in the Bible. It forms an Alephbetic link to 2 Kings. The word lekhu is the plural imperative of the Hé word halak (walk). It means both to come and to go, the latter being how it is used twice in the opening passage of 2 Kings below. The word li (to me) shows how Lamed combines with the Yod (sign of me or mine). The word translated as "I will teach you" exemplifies both the verb lamad and the Aleph prefix as the sign of "I will", and banim is the plural of the Beyth word ben (son). Its message closely echoes the call of י ה ו ה ב ן י ה ו ה unto each of us:

"Come unto me, all ye that labour and are heavy laden, and I will give you rest. Take my yoke upon you, and learn of me; for I am meek and lowly in heart: and ye shall find rest unto your souls. For my yoke is easy, and my burden is light."—Matthew 11:28

The idea of learning involves both positive and negative commandments, the latter being expressed by the fundamental Lamed word lo which means no or not. It is called the negative particle and is used in every "thou shalt not" found in the Ten Commandments. In this word, Aleph functions as a place holder for the vowel so its meaning as "no" comes primarily from the elemental force of Lamed as the sign of the rod of the teacher. י ה ו ה used this word in three Alephbetic Verses (Lamentations 1:12, 4:12; Proverbs 31:21).

This is the essence of the twelfth letter. It represents teaching and learning. It is the rod of the teacher that points his disciples towards truth and away from error. The miracle of י ה ו ה is that its symbolic meaning coheres precisely with its grammatical function as the sign of the prepositions "to," "for" and "so forth". This is the supernatural self-reflective integrity that unites the Hebrew Language with its Aleph-bets. The Twenty-Two Letters carry their distinct and unique meanings into the words that they form. Yet there is more! י ה ו ה used the symbolic meaning of Lamed as an absolutely unmistakable marker to identify a singular event in the biography of His Son י ה ו ה ב ן י ה ו ה, the greatest Teacher ever to live.

The image of the letter Lamed is a ox-goad, and is considered to have no other meaning. To me, Lamed refers to knowledge in all experiences on the physical plane of existence. This is the knowledge necessary to attain detachment from this world, making a bridge to other world by means of sacrifice.

Mem is the symbolic waters with the numerical value of forty. It represents morality and people. Mem is consciousness. Consciousness is the Primordial State of existence, it is the origin of all things, physical and subtle matter, of which thoughts are composed. It is the underlying substance behind all things: matter, thoughts, and energy. It is the Primeval Waters.

"For the earth shall be filled with the knowledge of the glory of the LORD יהוה, as the waters (mayim) cover the sea."—Habakkuk 2:14

The name of the thirteenth letter is based on the word mayim, meaning water. In the ancient Hebrew script, the pictograph for Mem was drawn as a wavy line indicating waves of water and is still seen in the Latin M. When written at the end of a word, it takes the final form—ם—which is more square, and smooth like calm water. The word table displays its profound connection with the meaning of its name. God used four of these words to describe the Flood of Noah, the greatest hydrological event in the history of the world:

"For yet seven days, and I will cause it to rain (matar) upon the earth forty days and forty nights; and every living substance that I have made will I destroy from off the face of the earth. And Noah did according unto all that the Lord יהוה commanded him. And Noah was six hundred years old when the flood of waters was upon the earth. And Noah went in, and his sons, and his wife, and his sons' wives with him, into the ark, because of the waters of the flood. And it came to pass after seven days, that the

waters (mayim) of the flood (mabul) were upon the earth. In the six
hundredth year of Noah's life, in the second month, the seventeenth day of
the month, the same day were all the fountains (ma'ayin) of the great deep
broken up, and the windows of heaven were opened."—Genesis 7:4-7, 10-
11

The flood also is one of the greatest events in the Bible. It is a
precursor (type) of the Universal Judgment that awaits till the End of
Time (Revelation 20:12). This is the Divine Judgment יהוה בן יהוה
suffered for us when He was "baptized" (Luke 12:50) on the Cross, and so
it is that water baptism that symbolizes our union with Him in His death,
burial, and resurrection (Romans 6:4). Scripture therefore declares Baptism
to be the antitype (fulfillment) corresponding to the type (foreshadow) of
the Flood (1 Peter 3:20). Just as the Flood cleansed the ancient world of
sinners, so we are cleansed by entering יהוה בן יהוה בן יהוה
through faith, symbolized by Baptism. Both symbols are also linked with
the Dove. All three fit together like pieces of a puzzle to form a threefold
unity. As a group, they are independent, but the Bible never links all three
at once, but there are many verses that link them pair-wise. For example,
Genesis 8:11 links the Dove with the Flood, 1 Peter 3:20 links Baptism
with the Flood, and Matthew 3:16 links the Dove with Baptism. These
relations can be represented by a _Venn Diagram_. The three circles represent
the three symbols. The verses connecting the pairs are listed in the space
where the circles overlap. Together, they display a Divine unity that no
single Book of the Bible reveals by itself. This is why we must understand
the whole Bible before we can really understand its parts.

Genesis 8:11: "And the dove came in to him in the evening; and, lo, in her
mouth was an olive leaf plucked off: so Noah knew that the waters were
abated from off the earth."

1 Peter 3:18: "*For* יהוה בן יהוה *also hath once suffered for sins, the just for the unjust, that he might bring us to* יהוה, *being put to death in the flesh, but made alive by the Spirit: By which also he went and preached unto the spirits in prisons. Which sometime were disobedient, when once the longsuffering of* יהוה *waited in the days of Noah, while the ark was a preparing, wherein few, that is, eight souls were saved by water. The like figure (antitype) whereunto even baptism doth also now save us (not the putting away of the filth of the flesh, but the answer of a good conscience toward* יהוה), *by the resurrection of* יהוה בן יהוה."

Matthew 3:16: "*And* יהוה בן יהוה, *when he was baptized, went up straightway out of the water: and, lo, the heavens were opened unto him, and he saw the Spirit of* יהוה, *descending like a dove, and lighting upon him.*"

What's so impressive here is that the flood happened millennia before the Cross, yet it fits like a perfectly pre-designed puzzle piece to integrate with the Gospel that was yet to come! There are innumerable examples of structures like this in the Bible. This is why Paul said that Scripture "preached the Gospel to Abraham" (Galatians 3:8). The Bible is One Book designed by יהוה to proclaim One Message—the everlasting Gospel of יהוה בן יהוה! Obviously, such epoch-spanning semantic art could come only from Him who dwells in Eternity.

The first two symbols—Baptism and the Flood—are directly connected with water, whereas the third—the Dove—is connected via its relation to the Holy Spirit. This association appears throughout Scripture from the first chapter of Genesis where the "Spirit of יהוה moved on the face of the waters" to the last chapter of Revelation where the Spirit and the Bride say "let him that is athirst come. And whosoever will, let him take the water of life freely." This is the water of the Spirit that יהוה promised saying, "I will pour water (mayim) upon him that is thirsty ... I will pour

My Spirit upon thy seed" (Isaiah 44:3). יהוה בן יהוה *fulfilled this promise, saying "If any man thirst, let him come unto me, and drink. He that believeth on me, as the scripture hath said, out of his belly shall flow rivers of living water" (St. John 7:38).* יהוה בן יהוה בן יהוה *then explained that the water represented "the Spirit, which they that believe on him should receive." As an aside, this verse attests to the Divinity of* יהוה בן יהוה *since He called everyone to come to Him to drink the living water, and Scripture identifies the "fountain of living waters" with* יהוה *Himself (Jeremiah 17:13).*

The strong Biblical connection between water and life is familiar to every living creature since all life depends upon this element. Every day, we drink it, prepare our food with it, and cleanse ourselves with it. It is, therefore, a universal symbol of the source of life, refreshment, cleansing, restoration, and renewal. Thus, יהוה *promises to lead us beside still waters and to restore our souls (Psalm 23:2). He tells us that anyone who delights in His Word and continuously meditates in it "shall be like a tree planted by the rivers of water, that bringeth forth his fruit in his season; his leaf also shall not wither; and whatsoever he doeth shall prosper" (Psalm 1:3), and calls us to joyfully "draw water (mayim) out of the wells (maqor) of salvation" (Isaiah 12:3). He united all this as the ultimate symbol of the source of life that flows from Him when He identified Himself as "the fountain of living waters" in Jeremiah 17:13:*

"O LORD, יהוה *, the hope (miqveh) of* ישראל *, all that forsake thee shall be ashamed, and they that depart from me shall be written in the earth, because they have forsaken the LORD* יהוה *, the fountain of living waters (maqor mayim chayim)."*

This verse uses three Mem words, including miqveh (hope) which is based on the Qowph word qavah (to wait) prefixed with a Mem to form the substantive noun. The root verb also means to gather together and as such gives rise to another meaning of miqveh as a gathering of water. This is the name of the Jewish ritual bath which shares many symbolic overtones with Baptism (cleansing, conversion, renewal). Both of these words first appear on the Third Day of Creation in conjunction with mayim:

"And יהוה said, Let the waters (mayim) under the heaven be gathered together (qavah) unto one place, and let the dry land appear: and it was so. And יהוה called the dry land Earth; and the gathering together (miqveh) of the waters (mayim) called he Seas (Yamim): and יהוה saw that it was good."—Genesis 1:9-10

Note the close relation between the words yamim (seas) and mayim (water). Historically, Biblical scholars have seen a profound connection with the events of the Third Day, the Flood, Baptism, and the Character and Work of the Third Person of the Triune Cycle. Just as יהוה gathered the waters on the Third Day, so the Holy Spirit gathers the people of יהוה into one place in יהוה בן יהוה בן יהוה. The Book of Revelation explicitly confirms the validity of this in Revelation 17:15:

"And he saith unto me, The waters which thou sawest, where the whore sitteth, are peoples, and multitudes, and nations, and tongues."

The "whore" is a familiar symbol of false religion and faithless people which was seen in study of the Scripture. It contrasts with the Bride as the symbol of all believers who have been gathered into one Body in בן יהוה יהוה בן יהוה. The Septuagint amplifies this association by using the Greek word synagogue to describe the "one place" where the waters were gathered. Revelation 22:17:

"And the Spirit and the bride say, Come. And let him that heareth say, Come. And let him that is athirst come. And whosoever will, let him take the water (mayim) of life freely."

The image of the letter Mem is water. Like Hé , the traditional meaning of Mem is the mother, the origin, the sea, the waters, and everything that is fertile. Mem is the reformer of life by successive transformation and by the changes it causes. Mem assures the movement of life.

CHAPTER 14
NUN
[noon]
נ ו ן
Symbolic: Fish Numerical Value: 50

Nun is the symbolic fish with the numerical value of fifty. It represents the soul, the physical human existence(below spiritual consciousness), where the higher nature (soul) is overcome by the lower nature (ego) and illusion of duality, individualism, pleasure, desire, ignorance, greed, emotionalism, passion, and sexuality. A state of spiritual death: "The Sting of Death," through the study of Torah and application, meditation, prayer, and fast; we can overcome "The Sting of Nun."

"יהוה בן יהוה בן יהוה the same yesterday, and to day, and for ever."—Hebrews 13:8

The name of the fourteenth letter is both a verb and a noun. As a verb, it means to continue, flourish, increase, sprout, or propagate. It appears this way only once in Scripture, in the great prophecy declaring the eternal endurance of the name of the Lord יהוה בן יהוה בן יהוה :

"His name shall endure for ever: his name shall be continued (yinon) as long as the sun: and men shall be blessed in him: all nations shall call him blessed."—Psalm 72:17

The Jews have long recognized the messianic character of this Psalm. The Talmud notes that when yinon is read as a noun, the verse can be understood as saying "His name shall endure forever; his name has been Yinon since before the sun was created." This was an early glimpse of the eternal nature of the Messiah, a central theme of the Book of Hebrews. This has endured to the present day, and appears in every commentary on the Hebrew Aleph-bets I have encountered.

As a noun, Nun means both perpetuity and posterity, the latter arising from the continuance of the family line. This manifests in the cognate neen (son/offspring), which appears three times in Scripture, always in conjunction with another word of similar meaning, neked (posterity). Rabbi Munk, in his book <u>Wisdom of the Hebrew Alphabet</u>, commented on the relation between neen and Nun in his section titled "The Word Nun Means Perpetuation," which he followed with a section called "The Everlasting Nun." This understanding is universal in the letter Nun as the symbol of posterity, perpetuity, and eternality. The word nun also denotes a fish because it is so prolific. Most dictionaries list this as the meaning of its name.

יהוה united the idea of posterity with the number fourteen in the structure of Matthew's genealogy of יהוה בן יהוה בן יהוה:

"So all the generations from Abraham to David are fourteen generations; and from David until the carrying away into Babylon are fourteen generations; and from the carrying away into Babylon unto יהוה בן יהוה בן יהוה are fourteen generations."—Matthew 1:17

The amazing thing is that יהוה also combined the Babylonian Exile with the Number 14 in the correlated substructure marked by the end of the pre-exilic Books of both 2 Chronicles) and Zephaniah, so that Written Word exhibits the same united thematic and numerical pattern as the genealogy of the Living Word!

The continuity, perpetuity, and posterity naturally flow into another set of fundamental words that originates in the great Alephbetic Psalm 119:111:

"Thy testimonies have I taken as an heritage (nachal) for ever: for they are the rejoicing of my heart."

This word is an exact pun on nachal (river), which paints the picture of a heritage as flowing like a river from one generation to the next. This logically extends the metaphor of people as water (Mem, water, people). It also encapsulates one of the most significant themes of the Book of Hebrews: יהוה בן יהוה בן יהוה as Heir of all things. Finally, all these ideas combine to form a picture of true faithfulness, which Webster's Dictionary aptly defines as "steadfast in allegiance, loyal, firm in adherence to promises or in observance of duty." This word appears in two of Alephbetic Verse: Psalm 111:7:

"The works of thy hands are verity and judgment; all his commandments are sure (ne'eman)."

Ne'eman means steadfast, sure, firm, trustworthy and faithful. It is based on the Aleph word emunah (faith). Scripture uses ne'eman to describe our "faithful God יהוה" (Deuteronomy 7:9), His servant Moshe whom He said "was faithful in all my house" (Numbers 12:7), and יהוה בן יהוה as the prophesied "faithful priest" (1 Samuel 2:35). It defines the central theological emphasis of both 2 Chronicles and Hebrews. These are seen in their utmost clarity in the articles יהוה בן יהוה: High Priest and Heir of All Things and A Priest Forever after the Order of Melchizedek.

The image of the letter Nun is a fish. A fish is one with its environment and has a spherical way of perception. This is a reference to the Astral Body and Astral World which symbol has always been the element Water. By contrast the element Earth refers to the Physical Plane of existence. Nun refers to universal life, changing continuously but always remaining the same just as the flowing waters.

<u>CHAPTER 15</u>
<u>SAMECH</u>
[saw'-mek]
ס מ ך
Symbolic: Prop or Support Numerical Value: 60

Samek is the symbolic prop with a numerical value of sixty. It represents giving and receiving with a pure heart filled with compassion, mercy, charity, respect, and love which is unity in the oneness of י ה ו ה.

"Humble yourselves in the sight of the Lord י ה ו ה ב ן י ה ו ה ב ן י ה ו ה, and he shall lift you up."—James 4:10

The name of the fifteenth letter Samek comes from the verb samak, variously translated in the KJV as support, uphold, sustain, establish, and stand fast. This coheres with its form in the ancient Hebrew script as a pillar upholding three horizontal beams. י ה ו ה firmly established its name and meaning in four Alephbetic Verses:

Psalm 145:14: "The LORD י ה ו ה upholdeth (samak) all that fall, and raiseth up all those that be bowed down."

Psalm 111:8a: "They stand fast (samak) for ever and ever......"

Psalm 112:8a: "His heart is established (samak), he shall not be afraid....."

Psalm 119:116: "Uphold (samak) me according unto thy word, that I may live: and let me not be ashamed of my hope."

As a verb, samak refers to all kinds of support—spiritual, moral, financial, and physical. It describes the support and foundation of buildings, as with "the two middle pillars upon which the house stood, and on which it was borne up (samak)" in the house brought down by Samson (Judges 16:29). יהוה presented the synonym sa'ad—typically translated with similar words such as uphold, support, sustain, help – as a word in Psalm 119:17:

"Hold thou me up (sa'ad), and I shall be safe: and I will have respect unto thy statutes continually."

יהוה used this word to metaphorically describe the foundation of a righteous king's throne, "Mercy and truth preserve the king: and his throne is upheld (sa'ad) by mercy" (Proverbs 20:28), and again in the prophecy of the Everlasting Kingdom of His Son, יהוה בן יהוה in Isaiah 9:6-

"For unto us a child is born, unto us a son is given: and the government shall be upon his shoulder: and his name shall be called Wonderful, Counselor, The mighty God, יהוה בן יהוה, The everlasting Father, The Prince of Peace. Of the increase of his government and peace there shall be no end, upon the throne of David, and upon his kingdom, to order it, and to establish (sa'ad) it with judgment and with justice from henceforth even for ever. The zeal of the LORD יהוה of hosts will perform this."

This word also appears in Ezra when יהוה sent the Prophet Haggai and others to help (sa'ad) the captives returning from the Babylonian Exile in their efforts to rebuild His Temple in Ezra 5:1-2:

"Then the prophets, Haggai the prophet, and Zechariah the son of Iddo, prophesied unto the Jews that were in Judah and Jerusalem in the name of the God of ישראל, even unto them. Then rose up Zerubbabel the son of Shealtiel, and Jeshua the son of Jozadak, and began to build the house of יהוה which is at Jerusalem: and with them were the prophets of יהוה

helping (sa'ad) them."

The third word listed in the table, sabal, also appears in Ezra when the gentile king Cyrus wrote his Decree of Support for the rebuilding of the Temple in Ezra 6:3:

"In the first year of Cyrus the king, the same Cyrus the king made a decree concerning the house of יהוה at Jerusalem, Let the house be builded, the place where they offered sacrifices, and let the foundations thereof be strongly laid (sabal); the height thereof threescore cubits, and the breadth thereof threescore cubits."

We are now beholding a supernatural threefold cord woven from 1). the meaning of Samek as support, 2). a main theme of the fifteenth Book, support for rebuilding of the Temple and Jerusalem, and 3). the first appearance of the Prophet Haggai, which he appears in no other Book. Yet this is but the beginning of wonders; the name of the fifteenth Book is itself is a synonym of Samek!

The image of the letter Samech is a prop, or support. Samech is both that what strains the string of the bow, and the humming of the string. Samech is also the hissing of a snake (through the idea of its pronunciation), the physical life force, the egotistic impulses, and the seductive instincts. Giving way to the lower nature energies and the snake pulls you down. However, they can be transformed, and the snake will pull you upwards. As a prop it is the life force that sustains everything, through that process it links the so above with the so below. The prop is also the spinal column or chord through which the life fluid flows and Kundalini serpent rises.

CHAPTER 16
'AYIN
[ah'-yin]
ע י ן
Symbolic: Eye Numerical Value: 70

Ayin is the symbolic eye with the numerical value of seventy. It represents eternity, concealment, that Primordial State of Consciousness of non-duality from which all existence arises, and to which all must return. It is the third eye that is connected to the higher senses of intuition, telepathy, psychometric, and clairvoyance.

The Eyes of י ה ו ה

"For who hath despised the day of small things? for they shall rejoice, and shall see the plummet in the hand of Zerubbabel with those seven; they are the eyes of the LORD י ה ו ה , which run to and fro through the whole earth."—Zechariah 4:10

The great themes of Scripture flow directly from the literal meaning of the name of the sixteenth letter—Ayin—the common Hebrew word for an eye, the organ of sight. This coheres with shape in the ancient script—O—a simple image of the eye. Ayin also denotes a well, spring, or fountain, a kind of "eye of water" in the ground. It is one of the most firmly established names; there being six Alephbetic Verses bearing witness to it: Psalm 25:15, 34:15, 119:123, 145:15 and Lamentations 3:49, 51.

The reference to "the eyes of the Lord י ה ו ה " in the last verse is exceedingly powerful. This phrase appears twenty-two times in the King James Version Bible, with the final two aligned with Zechariah 4:10 and this verse from 1 Peter 3:12:

"For the eyes of the Lord י ה ו ה *are over the righteous, and his ears are open unto their prayers: but the face of the Lord* י ה ו ה *is against them that do evil."*

     This verse from 1 Peter is a direct quote from the Ayin verse of Psalm 34. It is quoted in no other Book and so forms a unique link—an Alephbetic link from the Ayin verse of Psalm 34 to 1 Peter. Furthermore, the link is based on the meaning of the name of Ayin itself! Consider what is going on here. We have another top-level, super-obvious, explicit integration of the order of the Books of the Bible with the pattern of the Hebrew Aleph-bets.

     A closer analysis reveals a very tight connection between Psalm 34:15, and the literal meaning of the name of the letter Ayin. The exact phrase that appears in Zechariah 4:10 is einei י ה ו ה. This phrase appears in only six verses from four books (Deuteronomy 11:12, Psalm 34:15, Proverbs 5:21, 15:3, 22:12, Zechariah 4:10). When translated into the Greek Septuagint, the phrase became "opthalmoi kuriou" which appears in one and only one verse of the New Testament, (1 Peter 3:12). Much more common is the phrase b'einei י ה ו ה formed with the Beyth prefix to indicate the preposition "in". This phrase appears 92 times in Scripture, translated as "in the eyes of י ה ו ה " 13 times and "in the sight of י ה ו ה " 79 times.

     We have therefore and extremely strong thematic link from the Ayin verse of Psalm 34:15 to both Zechariah and 1 Peter. It is not an Alephbetic link to Zechariah because there is not a unique linking set as there is between it and 1 Peter 3:12 where it is quoted.

     This is an example of the astounding wealth of Alephbetic links found in Psalm 34. But the best is yet to come in the absolutely stunning Alephbetic link from the prophecy of the Crucifixion in its Shin verse to the unique record of its fulfillment in St. John's Gospel.

       The image of the letter Ayin is an eye. It signifies the source and nothingness from which everything emanated. It is also destruction by antagonism. It's expressed by winds and heavy sounds, and especially the image of emptiness. Ayin is the principle of the individuals revolt through materialism and putting importance on sensory satisfaction.

CHAPTER 17
PÉ
[pay]
פ ה
Symbolic: Mouth Numerical Value: 80

Pé is the symbolic mouth with the numerical value of eighty. It represents the power of intellect through words. Sound vibrations in the universe. It can alter consciousness and connect us to higher planes of existence. Through sound vibration of words י ה ו ה seventy-two names of power are brought forth to aid us in our earthly journey.

"The law of truth was in his mouth (Pé), and iniquity was not found in his lips: he walked with me in peace and equity, and did turn many away from iniquity. For the priest's lips should keep knowledge, and they should seek the law at his mouth (Pé): for he is the messenger of the LORD י ה ו ה of hosts."—Malachi 2:6-7

The name of the seventeenth letter signifies the mouth, the organ of speech. י ה ו ה used it as a word in three Alephbetic Verses, two of which are followed by the closely associated words patach and pa'ar, both translated as open:

Psalm 37:30: "The mouth (Pé) of the righteous speaketh wisdom, and his tongue talketh of judgment."

Proverbs 31:26: "She openeth (patach) her mouth (Pé) with wisdom; and in her tongue is the law of kindness."

Psalm 119:131: "I opened (pa'ar) my mouth (Pé), and panted: for I longed for thy commandments."

The alliterative repetition of Pé words emphasizes and amplifies its symbolic meaning by showing how this Letter links related ideas. This is very common in the Aleph-betic Verses as seen, for example, with Bet, Teyth, and Tsaddi. י ה ו ה also used the verb patach (to open) and its associated noun petach (entrance) as words in two other Alephbetic Verses:

Psalm 145:16: "Thou openest (patach) thine hand, and satisfiest the desire of every living thing."

Psalm 119:130: "The entrance (petach) of thy words giveth light; it giveth understanding unto the simple."

Christians are familiar with patach through its Aramaic cognate preserved in Mark 7:34:

"And looking up to heaven, he sighed, and saith unto him, Ephphatha, that is, Be opened."

This word uses the soft Phe—פ—that sounds like "f" or "ph." It is distinguished from the hard Pé—פ—by the dot (dagesh) in the center. This letter is also one of the five that take an alternate final (sofet) form—ף— when written at the end of a word. The hard Pé is called explosive because its sound is made by suddenly bursting open the lips to release the pressure behind them. Its elementary power is clearly displayed in the word puach (puff, blow). Both it and its translation puff are onomatopoetic (they sound like what they describe). This sets the tone for many of the prominent themes most notable by the prophecies of the Parousia, the Coming of the Lord י ה ו ה. י ה ו ה ב ן י ה ו ה ב ן י ה ו ה. The idea of opening is amplified yet again in another word that י ה ו ה used twice in conjunction with Pé:

Lamentations 2:16: "All thine enemies have opened (patzah) their mouth (Pé) against thee."

Lamentations 3:46: "All our enemies have opened (patzah) their mouths (Pé) against us."

Note again the alliteration of Pé words, including the name of the letter itself. Almost all occurrences of patzah, describe opening the mouth. Its first appearance is in conjunction with Pé and another very important word—panim (face)—when יהוה cursed Cain after he had murdered our righteous brother Abel:

"And now art thou cursed from the earth, which hath opened (patzah) her mouth (Pé) to receive thy brother's blood from thy hand. And Cain said unto the LORD יהוה , My punishment is greater than I can bear. Behold, thou hast driven me out this day from the face (panim) of the earth; and from thy face (panim) shall I be hid (essater); and I shall be a fugitive and a vagabond in the earth; and it shall come to pass, that every one that findeth me shall slay me."—Genesis 4:11, 13, 14

Cain's cry that he would be hid from יהוה 's face is an essential key to the Book of Esther. The verb translated "I will be hid"–(essater)–is spelt with exactly the same letters as (Esther), differing only in two vowel points. As an aside, this exemplifies the Aleph prefix as the sign of "I will." The name of the Book of Esther therefore points directly to one of its most powerful Secrets of the Triune God—it contains no mention of יהוה whatsoever! Read it! This is a very rare and powerful secret, found in no other Book except the Song of Songs, and is one of the reasons its inclusion in the Canon was strongly debated. As we shall see, יהוה 's apparent absence is an essential aspect of Esther which He designed to demonstrate His providential care even when He seems to be absent, "hiding His face" as it were. This is an example of the overwhelming power of the Bible to explain long-standing controversies.

The word panim (face) is from the root panah (turn, look) in the sense that you see the face when someone turns to look at you. It is evident in the name Peniel (Face of God) that Jacob coined after he wrestled with יהוה, saying "for I have seen יהוה face to face" (panim el panim, Genesis 32:30). יהוה used these words in five Alephbetic Verses:

Psalm 25:16: "Turn (panah) thee unto me, and have mercy upon me; for I am desolate and afflicted."

Psalm 119:132: "Look (panah) thou upon me, and be merciful unto me, as thou usest to do unto those that love thy name."

Ps 119:135: "Make thy face (panim) to shine upon thy servant; and teach me thy statutes."

Psalm 34:16: "The face (panim) of the LORD יהוה is against them that do evil, to cut off the remembrance of them from the earth."

Lamentations 4:16 "The face (panim) of the LORD יהוה hath divided them; he will no more regard them: they respected not the persons of the priests, they favoured not the elders."

The most frequent use of panim is in its construct state p'nei (face of) with the Lamed prefix the sign of the prepositions to or for, form liphnei which literally means "to the face of" and is usually translated as "in front of," "before," "towards," or "in the presence of." The frequency of this word is greatly maximized in Esther where it plays an essential role in the overall structure of the story which begins with Vashti's refusal to show off her beauty "before (liphnei) the king ... the people and the princes" (1:11), and climaxes when Esther boldly, and at her own peril, presents herself "before (liphnei) the king" to save her people from destruction (8:4).

As often happens, the original word order was lost in translation. The alliteration is seen in the transliterated Hebrew which begins in both cases with conjugations of the word Pé, and reads Piah petach (Her mouth she opens) and Pi pa'arti (My mouth I opened). The word piah is the construct form of Pé suffixed with the fifth Letter Hé to signify the feminine possessive, her mouth. Likewise, the word pi is the construct form of Pé suffixed with Yod to indicate first person possessive, and pa'arti is the first person qal perfect conjugation of pa'ar (open).

The image of the letter Pé is the mouth. But the mouth can be considered as an a opening out of which breath comes, or the Breath of Life. Thus Pé can been seen as an a opening for the Light of Higher SELf shines forth. Here man finally perceives his higher being and brings his consciousness in alignment with it. When consciousness remains in this brilliant light, the light itself becomes of well out of which energy, light, knowledge and wisdom is flowing. A well is like a mouth in the earth, giving us the water of life.

<u>CHAPTER 18</u>
<u>TSADDI</u>
[tsaw-day']
צ ד י
Symbolic: Fish Hook Numerical Value: 90

Tsaddi is the symbolic fish hook with a numerical value of ninety. It represents standing upright on the square of morality,
in the circle of spirituality, subtling the lower nature of (ego) and the sting of death: ignorance, individuality-ism, selfishness, extravagantness, wonton, sexuality, jealousy, envy, greed, gluttony, and hate. Through study one is initiated into the order of TSADDIK.

"My little children, these things write I unto you, that ye sin not. And if any man sin, we have an advocate with the Father, בן יהוה בן יהוה יהוה *the righteous.*"—*1 John 2:1*

יהוה *established the primary symbolic meaning of the eighteenth letter with great clarity in six Alephbetic Verses (Psalm 112:9, 119:137, 142, 144, 145:17 and Lamentations 1:18).*

יהוה *used this word when He declared the way of the Gospel, "the just (Tsaddi) shall live by faith" (Habakkuk 2:4), and again in the genesis of the Gospel when Abraham "believed in the Lord, and it was counted unto him as righteousness (tzedakah)" (Genesis 15:6). The link between righteousness and the eighteenth letter is ancient and fundamental. This uniformly attests to the understanding of Tsaddi, and to this day many Jews refer to the eighteenth letter by the name Tzaddik.*

All six of the Alephbetic Verses listed above refer to יהוה *'s perfect and eternal righteousness. He alone is, was, and ever will be Tzaddik. This is the uniform declaration of all Scripture. But how then do we understand* evil in the world? Why do the righteous suffer? Where is the Divine Counsel concerning the Problem of Evil in light of יהוה's Righteousness? This is the topic of the Book of Job, the first of the Five Wisdom Books.

The image of the letter Tsaddi is a small swath. Tsaddi symbolizes both hierarchical distribution and the universal matter in its crystallization. It is also the refuge of the being towards which the hopes are directed. Tsaddi can be considered as the creation of the physical, the senses, and illusions. Sometimes it is shown as the expression of the Divine Mother.

<u>CHAPTER 19</u>
<u>QOWPH</u>
[cofe]
ק ו ף
Symbolic: Back of the Head Numerical Value: 100

Qowph is the symbolic back of the head with a numerical value of one hundred. It represents memory and comprehension. Remembering to keep the Shabbat Holy. He or she who desecrates any of the commandments is regarded as a transgressor, while he or she who doesn't remember to keep the Shabbat Holy is considered as a heathen, denying the existence of י ה ו ה.

"I cried with my whole heart; hear me, O LORD, י ה ו ה: I will keep thy statutes. I cried unto thee; save me, and I shall keep thy testimonies."—Psalm 18:6

The name of the nineteenth letter denotes an Eye of a Needle. This coheres with its form in the ancient Hebrew script as a circle with a line descending from it. It's still seen in the modern form and the corresponding Latin Q, which looks like a piece of thread being threaded through the eye of a needle. Qowph is the most guttural of the twenty-two Hebrew Alephbets. Its sound originates deep in the back of the throat and is aptly described as the croaking of a crow's caw. This is the basis of the primary word qara (cry, call) which י ה ו ה used in many of the Qowph Alephbetic Verses(Psalm 119:145-146; Lamentations 1:19, 3:55).

Qara is onomatopoetic; it sounds like what it describes. Words with a similar meaning and sound appear in many languages, most notably the Greek krazw (kradzo, cry) which is often used to translate qara in the Septuagint. It is prominent in Mark's Gospel. י ה ו ה used a closely related word, qol (voice), twice in the Alephbetic Verses:

Psalm 119:149: Hear my voice (qol) according unto thy lovingkindness: O LORD י ה ו ה, quicken me according to thy judgment.

Lamentations 3:56: "Thou hast heard my voice (qol): hide not thine ear at my breathing, at my cry."

The Hebrew qol (voice, call) is phonetically similar to the Greek kalew (kaleo, call) and the corresponding English call. All these words and the ideas they represent are fundamental to the nature of the Book of Psalms, the Bible's great Guide to Prayer that teaches us how to call unto God. They appear together in many Psalms. Note that the quotes below are not Alephbetic Psalms. We are looking here at characteristic verses of the Nineteenth Book itself to discern its dominant message:

Psalm 3:4: "I cried (qara) unto the LORD י ה ו ה with my voice (qol), and he heard me out of his holy hill. Selah."

Psalm 27:7: "Hear, O LORD י ה ו ה, when I cry (qara) with my voice (qol): have mercy also upon me, and answer me."

Psalm 55:16-17: "As for me, I will call (qara) upon י ה ו ה; and the LORD י ה ו ה shall save me. Evening, and morning, and at noon, will I pray, and cry aloud: and he shall hear my voice (qol).

Psalm 141:1: "LORD, י ה ו ה, I cry (qara) unto thee: make haste unto me; give ear unto my voice (qol), when I cry (qara) unto thee."

These characteristic passages span the beginning, middle, and end of the Book of Psalms. They display the perfect integration of the position and content of Psalms with the position and symbolic meaning of the nineteenth letter.

The triliteral root qara is extremely common. It occurs 737 times in the Old Testament. Though I haven't found any real correlation between its raw distribution and structure, but I have found a highly significant correlation if we search for all first person occurrences of qara, as represented by the phrases in the set [I cry, I cried, I will cry, I have cried, I call, I called, I will call, I have called].

The great theme of the Psalms can now be easily seen to be an objective property of Scripture. Furthermore, this theme is integrated with the Hebrew Aleph-bets and the meaning of Qowph as presented by יהוה Himself in the great Alephbetic Psalm 119! Glory to יהוה in the highest!

The image of the letter Qowph is the back of the head. When the last wall has been torn down, the last veil torn away, the last spot of darkness removed, the Kundalini will rise up along the spine to the back of the head. Then the illumination happens. The light shines from within. Another image of Qowph is an ax. The ax has always been regarded as a divine tool because the ax is used for splitting. In the spiritual sense splitting releases the energy that lies in or behind the split object. Therefore the ax, especially the double headed ax, was used to indicate divine revelation or enlightenment.

CHAPTER 20

RESH

[raysh]

ר י ש

Symbolic: Head Numerical Value: 200

Resh is the symbolic head with a numerical value of two hundred. It represents a ruwach that possesses the four Hebrew virtues: Prudence, Temperance, Justice, and Fortitude; having balance between the higher and lower natures within self. Standing upright on Torah.

"The fear of the LORD יהוה is the beginning of wisdom: and the knowledge of the holy is understanding."—Proverbs 9:10

The name of the twentieth letter is a variation of common Hebrew words for the head (Resh). This coheres with its shape in the ancient script, a picture of the head atop the neck. When reversed, it became the Greek P (Rho) which evolved into the Latin R by having a leg added. Scripture attests to its name; יהוה used it in the last Resh verse of Psalm 119, the great Alephbetic Psalm praising His Word from Aleph to Thav; Psalm 119:160:

"Thy word is true from the beginning (Resh): and every one of thy righteous judgments endureth for ever."

As often happens, the original word order was lost in translation. In Hebrew, the opening clause reads "Resh davarkah emet" which literally means "the head (or beginning) of thy word is truth." But just as sum relates to summit and amount to mountain, so Resh denotes the top, sum, total, or amount of something, as in Psalm 139:17:

"How precious also are thy thoughts unto me, O יהוה! how great is the sum (Resh) of them!"

Many translations, such as the NASB, use this to render the verse as "The sum of thy word is truth." This conveys an important aspect of its meaning and preserves the proper word order. י ה ו ה used a closely related word in the Resh clause of Psalm 111, where again the King James Version Bible reversed the original word order which begins with the phrase reshith chokmah in Hebrew; Psalm 111:10 in part reads:

"The fear of the Lord י ה ו ה is the beginning of wisdom."

In all the Bible, the phrase reshith chokmah appears in one and only one other verse—Proverbs 4:7—the first instruction of the Ten Step Study Method—where reshith is translated as a principle thing and linked with Resh as head:

"Wisdom is the principal thing (reshith chokmah); therefore get wisdom: and with all thy getting get understanding. Exalt her, and she shall promote thee: she shall bring thee to honour, when thou dost embrace her. She shall give to thine head (Resh) an ornament of grace: a crown of glory shall she deliver to thee."—Proverbs 4:7-9

This passage sums up the heart and soul of the twentieth Book. Of the 234 references to wisdom in the Bible, nearly half appear in the Five Wisdom Books. And of those 113, nearly half again appear in Proverbs. It is the premier Book of Wisdom set as a jewel in the exact center of the Five Wisdom Books. We have here an extremely dense set of converging lines all focusing on one theme. It begins with the Alephbetic link from the Resh verse of Psalm 111 to Proverbs 4:7. The phrase—"the beginning of wisdom"—points to the central theme of the Book to which it links. The word itself—reshith—is based on the literal meaning of the twentieth letter—Resh (head)—thereby signifying the Seat of the Mind and Center of

Wisdom in we who bear the Image of יהוה. And as if this were not enough, the linked passage in Proverbs reiterates its own connection with Resh, saying that wisdom "shall give to thine head (Resh) an ornament of grace." This is beyond anything anyone could ever have imagined. The order and content of the Books track exactly with the order and symbolic meanings of the Hebrew Letters as presented by God Himself in the Alephbetic Verses, and all of this is locked in place with an unbreakable multifaceted link!

Yet there is still more. יהוה amplified the connection between Resh, Wisdom, and the twentieth Book in another verse—Proverbs 9:10. It contains the only other occurrence of the English phrase "the beginning of wisdom" in the King James Version Bible. The Hebrew is different but the idea is the same and is faithfully rendered as such. This means that we have two distinct links—one in Hebrew (Proverbs 4:7) and one in English—(Proverbs 9:10)—to the Resh verse of Psalm 111. The significance of this cannot be overstated. We now have a double Alephbetic link based on a Resh word that expresses the central theme of the twentieth Book and all of this is implicit in the meaning of Resh as a symbol the Head, the Seat of the Mind!

This is an extraordinary convergence of multiple independent lines onto a single point. It reveals, yet again, the full Divine integration of the order and meaning of the Hebrew Aleph-bets with that of the Books in the Canon. It is the limitless glory and detailed perfection of יהוה's Wisdom revealed in the structure of His Holy Word. It is one of the premier examples of an Alephbetic link which proves the Divine design of the whole Bible on the pattern of the Hebrew Aleph-bets.

The image of the letter Resh is a head. The head is where illumination takes place. Resh refers to the divine forces, the totality of the universe, to cosmic life in everywhere and in everything. Resh is the *movement of things by destruction and generation. The old is left and the new come forth.*

CHAPTER 21

SHIN

[sheen]

שׁ י ן

Symbolic: Fire or Tooth Numerical Value: 300

Shin is the symbolic fire with the numerical value of three hundred. It represents wisdom, intellectual wisdom, experiential wisdom, and intuitional (spiritual) wisdom. Shin symbolizes the Hebraic Triad of the first three Sephiroth on the Cosmic Tree of Life: Keter, Chochmah, and Binah. The three Elemental Forces of Creation: Fire (will), Air (intellect), and Water (emotion). The three levels of Consciousness: Conscious, Subconscious, and Unconsciousness. The three Worlds: Physical, Astral, and Causal. The three Modes of Nature: Dull, Agitated, and Lucid. The three Aspects of Adam's Experience: Seer, Seen, and Sight. And as well as the three stages of Initiation: Ignorance, Aspiration, and Enlightenment. Shin (fire) symbolizes the purification of the Mind, Body, and Soul. Most importantly Shin implies that wisdom, the light of Truth, illuminates and burns away ignorance, egoism, eradicates, and transforms mortal consciousness to immortal consciousness. Shin is also falsehood, slander, deceit, mastery in the lower nature which must be transformed into spiritual energy.

"Then spake יהוה בן יהוהבן יהוה again unto them, saying, I am the light of the world: he that followeth me shall not walk in darkness, but shall have the light of life."—John 8:12

The name of the twenty-first letter literally means a tooth. This is the origin of its form in the ancient script. Its name, pronounced "sheen," has two sounds; a dot above the left side indicates the "s" sound made by forcing air over the sharp edge of the teeth, and a dot above right side indicates the "sh" sound made by forcing air through the teeth. יהוה

established the name of Shin in Psalm 112:10 where you can watch the thematic flow of Psalm 112:10:

"[Resh] The wicked (rasha) shall see it, and be grieved; [Shin] he shall gnash with his teeth (shen), and melt away: [Thav] the desire (ta'avah) of the wicked shall perish."

Teeth frequently appear in Scripture as a natural symbol of things that bite, crush, and devour, as in Daniel's vision of the "dreadful and terrible" beast with "great iron teeth" that "devoured and brake in pieces" (Daniel 7:7). This then links to another Shin word in Psalm 10:15:

"Break (shavar) thou the arm of the wicked and the evil man: seek out his wickedness till thou find none."

The word shavar plays an important role in one of the most significant Alephbetic links found in the entire Bible. The great themes are based on the symbolic power of Shin which shines most clearly when combined with Aleph to form esh (fire). In its ultimate sense, this is the Fire of יהוה 's Glory that consumes and devours the wicked even as it purifies and enlightens the faithful. Shin carries this meaning into the word shemesh (sun)—the essence of fire and symbol of daylight—that shall reveal everyone's works in the Day of Judgment when we all shall see the face of יהוה בן יהוה בן יהוה shining "like the sun" (Revelation 1:16).

יהוה has revealed His Light in His Word. He instructed us to teach it "diligently" (Deuteronomy 6:7), using the word shanan which literally means to sharpen. This is the root of Shin (tooth) since teeth are sharp. In its literal sense, shanan speaks of whetting the edge of a sword or tip of an arrow, and is used figuratively for honing the intellect. יהוה amplified these ideas in Psalm 111:10 with the word sekel that denotes a sharp mind in Psalm 111:10:

[Resh] The fear of the LORD י ה ו ה is the beginning (reshith) of wisdom: [Shin] A good understanding (sekel) have all they that do his commandments: [Thav] his praise (tehillah) endureth for ever.

The thematic flow of this threefold passage contrasts the destiny of the faithful with that of the wicked outlined in Psalm 112:10. It shows how differently י ה ו ה's Light impacts the saints as compared to unrepentant sinners. This is a primary theme of St. John's Gospel: St. John 3:20:

"For every one that doeth evil hateth the light, neither cometh to the light, lest his deeds should be reproved. But he that doeth truth cometh to the light, that his deeds may be made manifest, that they are wrought in י ה ו ה.

The word sekel describes Daniel and his friends after "י ה ו ה" gave them knowledge and skill (sekel) in all learning and wisdom" (Daniel 1:17). It also describes the "wise" who "shall shine as the brightness of the firmament" in the Day of Judgment (Daniel 12:3). It's one of the many Hebrew roots that are strikingly similar to English words of the same meaning, having the same consonants in the same order. The Theological Dictionary of the New Testament contrasts its root verb sakal with the Beyth word bin.

In many instances sakal is synonymous with bin, but there is a fine distinction. While bin indicates "distinguishing between", sakal relates to an intelligent knowledge of the reason. There is the process of thinking through a complex arrangement of thoughts resulting in a wise dealing and use of good practical common sense. Bin relates to analysis; sakal to synthesis and comprehension. It is the light of understanding that dawns as all the puzzle-pieces fall into place and the image of the whole is seen, which should be happening now in the your mind as we approach the last Aleph-bet.

The image of the letter Shin is a tooth. The form of the letter Shin refers to the three roots of the molars. Shin has also the meaning of the Cosmic Fire or Fiery Spirit, the Holy Spirit. Because the tooth or molar refers to taking of food, to eating, to taking in, it indicates, in combination with its other meaning, the reception of the Cosmic Fire. It is the influx of the Holy Spirit that flowed into the heads of the Apostles, shown as a flame above each of their heads. The body has taken in the Fiery Spirit. This Fire os Shin is the dynamic movement in the universe and its active and expansive forces. With this fire ones dances on the world. Shin is the movement of everything that exists. Shin vivifies all beings great and small. It is the Cosmic Snake or the Cosmic Dragon. The shape of Shin also refers to the Triune Cycle, here in its fiery aspect, the descending Dove. Its shape is composed of three Wav's placed next to each other, giving the number 666, which is the number of the Sun, and also the number of the Beast in the Book of Revelation. The number 666 is not evil as it is often thought, it is a number of mystery. The three flames in the letter Shin are also explained as being the representation of the Od or the active force of life, the Ob or the passive force of life, and the Aur or the balancing force of life.

CHAPTER 22

THAV

[thawv]

ת ו

Symbolic: Mark or Sign Numerical Value: 400

Thav is the symbolic Mark with a numerical value of four hundred. It represents life and death, blessings and coursings'. It is a sign of ♂ male, ♀ female of life and blessing, being י ה ו ה , in keeping the Shabbat and the laws, statutes, judgments, and commandments contained in the Book of Torah. Being scaled with the mark of Zayin in your head and on your hands, numerical value seven; Head (spiritual mind-set) and Hand (righteous works). It is the sign of death; being of the beast in not keeping the Sabbath. Being sealed with the mark of Wav numerical value six on your head (materialistic mind-set) and on your hands (unrighteous works). Thav is the seal of truth, for it is the mark on the forehead of the faithful one who have thrived to keep the law of HA-TORAH from ALÊPH to THÂV. Thav is also the seal of death, for it is the word to appear in the word DEATH: מ ו ת (MAWETH).

"And I saw in the right hand of him that sat on the throne a book written within and on the backside, sealed with seven seals. And I saw a strong angel proclaiming with a loud voice, Who is worthy to open the book, and to loose the seals thereof?"—Revelation 5:1

י ה ו ה designed the symbolic meaning of the twenty-two Hebrew Aleph-bets to proclaim the message of the everlasting Gospel. The meaning of each letter derives from its name, position in the Aleph-bets, grammatical function and associated words. The meaning of the last Aleph-bet is very plain; and have agreed about it from the beginning. As noted, its name (Thav) is a common Hebrew word that denotes a mark, sign, or cross. In the ancient Hebrew script, it was written alternately as or the latter being

identical to the traditional form of the Cross of בן יהוה בן יהוה
יהוה. *It is the origin of the corresponding Greek Tau and Latin T.* יהוה
displayed its primary symbolic meaning in two Alephbetic Verses:

*Psalm 25:21: "Let integrity (tom) and uprightness preserve me; for I wait
on thee."*

*Lamentations 4:22: "The punishment of thine iniquity is accomplished
(tamam), O daughter of Zion; he will no more carry thee away into
captivity: he will visit thine iniquity, O daughter of Edom; he will discover
thy sins."*

*This is the glorious wonder of the Secrets of the Triune God; it is
self-evidently perfect from beginning to end. Thav, the final Aleph-bet that
completes and seals the entire Bible.* יהוה *placed it in the Alephbetic
Verses as signs that prophetically anticipated the flawless integrity of His
Word as a whole! Yet there is more, so much more. Thav is called the Seal
of Truth, and its form as a cross returns us to the central theme of all
Scripture, the Gospel of* יהוה בן יהוה בן יהוה *who sealed our
salvation and bought us by the blood of His Cross!*

*Moreover, the Hebrew scholar Gesenius noted that Thav was "a sign
in the form of a cross branded on the thigh or neck of horses and camels."
The form of the cross itself is the archetypal seal and elemental sign of
ownership.* יהוה *Himself used it to identity His faithful Remnant in a
vision He gave to the Prophet Ezekiel:*

"And the Lord יהוה *said, Go through the midst of the city, through the
midst of Jerusalem, and set a mark (Thav) upon the foreheads of the men
that sigh and that cry for all the abominations that be done in the midst
thereof. And to the others he said in mine hearing, Go ye after him through
the city, and smite: let not your eye spare, neither have ye pity: Slay utterly*

old and young, both maids, and little children, and women: but come not near any man upon whom is the mark (Thav); and begin at my sanctuary. Then they began at the ancient men which were before the house."—Ezekiel 9:4-6

The actual Hebrew word translated as mark in this verse is Thav, the name of the Twenty-Second Letter. Everyone marked with the Thav Cross was protected when יהוה poured out his wrath on the apostates corrupting His Temple. Similar imagery appears in Revelation 7 when יהוה sealed 144,000 of His servants in their foreheads against the coming judgment. All of this conspires to reveal Thav as the Covenant Aleph-bet which is the meaning recognized since antiquity. It is here that we come to an ultimate understanding of the overall structure of Scripture and an answer to the question: Why is the entire Bible built upon the number 22? It is the Divine Seal of Scripture—a perfect Circle, sevenfold symmetric perfection, sealed with the Cross! Could anything be simpler? Could anything be more beautiful?

The ancients calls Thav the Seal of יהוה, the Seal of Truth, and the Seal of Creation. The last letter or seal of the word emet, "truth," itself—the seal of יהוה's seal is the letter Thav, simple faith, the conclusion and culmination of all twenty-two forces—Aleph-bets—active in Creation.

Could the truth shine forth more plainly? Could יהוה have made it any simpler? For nearly two thousand years the truth of יהוה has been lifted high upon the steeples throughout the world. It is the sign of the Cross!

Emet (truth) also is an anagram of m'eth, which can be read as From Aleph-Thav; coheres with the universal intuition expressed in such words a "I swear to tell the truth, the whole truth, and nothing but the truth, so help me יהוה." Truth falls short if it includes less than the whole, from

Aleph to Thav. Likewise, all truth ultimately comes from יהוה, who identifies Himself as the beginning and the end, which is the Aleph and the Thav. It is the eternal foundation of the biblical structure.

Thav, יהוה's Seal, governs the twenty-two Aleph-bets. This manifests in the distribution of words cognate with "seal". This represents the result of searching the entire King James Bible for all such occurrences.

The vast majority of occurrences of seal and its cognates in the Bible come from its last book. This is because Revelation describes both the opening of the book "sealed with seven seals "(Revelation 5:1) and the sealing of the 144,000 from the tribes of ישראל with "the seal of the living God, יהוה" (Revelation 7:2). The significance of this word distribution can not be overstated. It is a simple demonstration of יהוה's careful design of the Bible in accordance with the structure and symbolic meaning of the Hebrew Aleph-bets as revealed in the text of Scripture.

The last book of the Bible prefigures the great themes found in the last book of the Bible. Just as Revelation explicitly proclaims a promise of everlasting life for the faithful and a warning of fiery judgment for the unbelievers, so ends the verses of the Song of Solomon 8:6-7:

"Set me as a seal upon thine heart, as a seal upon thine arm: for love is strong as death; jealousy is cruel as the grave: the coals thereof are coals of fire, which hath a most vehement flame. Many waters cannot quench love, neither can the floods drown it: if a man would give all the substance of his house for love, it would utterly be contemned."

The links between Love, Death, and יהוה's Seal are many and profound. As it is written in St John 15:13:

"Greater love hath no man than this, that a man lay down his life for his *friends."*

And again in Matthew 16:24-26:

"If any man will come after me, let him deny himself, and take up his cross, and follow me. For whosoever will save his life shall lose it: and whosoever will lose his life for my sake shall find it. For what is a man profited, if he shall gain the whole world, and lose his own soul? or what shall a man give in exchange for his soul?"

And in the most significant sense, יהוה בן יהוהבן יהוה *spoke of His own death as his glorification, and His great work that He came into the world to accomplish. It was on His Cross that He sealed the New Covenant of our Eternal Salvation with His own blood. Thus it was from His Cross that He declared, IT IS FINISHED (St. John 19:30)*

The image of the letter Thav is a cross Mark. The cross is a very ancient symbol, its most basic meaning is that of the division of the universe into four directions, by this it encloses the universe in its entirety. Thav is regarded as a symbol for the absolute, the perfection of creation. Thav is the summary of everything in everything. As the hundreds of the Hebrew Aleph-bets represents the Physical World, Thav, as the last Aleph-bet, represents the furthest development in the Physical World. Its numerical value is four hundred, and it is used to indicate infinity.

NOTES

NOTES

NOTES

NOTES